"I wonder why I don't believe you?"

Olivia didn't even blush. "What does it matter? Are we all set to go?"

"We're not going anywhere. Did you really think that you could get away with this ploy? Do you think I don't see through it?"

"What do you mean?"

The direct question took him by surprise. Nick's eyebrows drew into a frown and he let go of her arm. His jaw tightened and he said shortly, "There's nothing between us any longer, Olivia. It's over. Finished. I stopped feeling anything for you long ago."

It was cruel and it was meant to be. But Olivia had expected nothing less and didn't even flinch.

Dear Reader,

We know from your letters that many of you enjoy traveling to foreign locations—especially from the comfort of your favorite chair. Well, sit back, put your feet up and let Harlequin Presents take you on a yearlong tour of Europe. **Postcards from Europe** will feature a special title every month, set in one of your favorite European countries, written by one of your favorite Harlequin Presents authors. This month, discover some hidden corners of Shakespeare's "scepter'd isle"—England. Join Nick and Olivia as they explore Stratford-upon-Avon, the Cotswolds *and* their true feelings for each other.

The Editors

P.S. Don't miss the fascinating facts we've compiled about England. You'll find them at the end of the story.

HARLEQUIN PRESENTS

Postcards from Europe

SALLY WENTWORTH

Yesterday's Affair

Harlequin Books

TORONTO • NEW YORK • LONDON
AMSTERDAM • PARIS • SYDNEY • HAMBURG
STOCKHOLM • ATHENS • TOKYO • MILAN
MADRID • WARSAW • BUDAPEST • AUCKLAND

ISBN 0-373-11668-3

YESTERDAY'S AFFAIR

Copyright © 1992 by Sally Wentworth.

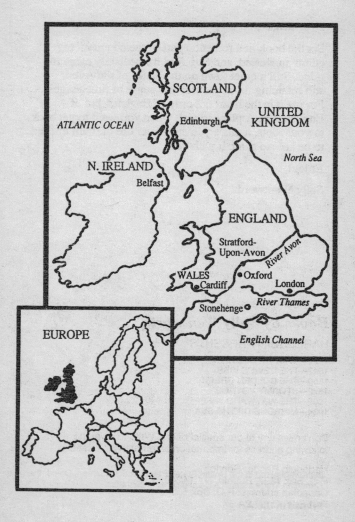

Dear Reader,

"Set the book in a romantic part of the country," my editor suggested, and Stratford immediately came to mind. Still a quiet town on the banks of the Avon, still retaining its old houses and sense of timelessness. For me it is the heart not only of England, but of Englishness. A place to visit when you want to get back to your roots, a place you can never tire of. I am thrilled to be able to share it with you.

Enjoy!

Sally Wentworth

Books by Sally Wentworth

HARLEQUIN PRESENTS

Don't miss any of our special offers. Write to us at the following address for information on our newest releases.

Harlequin Reader Service
P.O. Box 1397, Buffalo, NY 14240
Canadian address: P.O. Box 603,
Fort Erie, Ont. L2A 5X3

CHAPTER ONE

GLANCING down at the luggage overflowing the airport trolley, Olivia Grant decided that there was no way she could cope with it all on the subway into London. It would have to be a cab and to hell with the expense. Automatic doors opened in front of her, letting in a breath of fresh March air as she left the terminal building and headed for the cab rank. There was a line of taxis waiting for fares. They were square, black and stately, making the yellow cabs back in New York look like frantic sports cars in comparison. The sight of them gave Olivia a *frisson* of excitement; every film she'd ever seen about London had featured a London taxi—they were far too grand to be called cabs—and for the first time she really felt that she was in a strange country, a strange continent.

A driver whose accent sounded so Cockney that he must have been born right under Bow bells, never mind in sound of them, cheerfully lifted her luggage inside on to the floor, but her lap-top computer she kept on the seat beside her. Although the air was chill the sun was shining brightly, catching Olivia's eyes as they emerged into the open, so that she had to put up a hand to shield them as she looked eagerly out of the windows.

So this was England, this green land of absurdly small fields and leafless trees. Nick's England, that he had spoken of with unknowing pride and nostalgia. She had always wanted to come here, of course, but listening to him had fired her imagination even more. She would have come anyway, she told herself, even if she hadn't wanted to see Nick again so badly. After they'd split up and he'd gone back to England he had answered her first few letters, but then had come a long gap when he hadn't replied, and finally, appallingly, a last letter only to say that he thought it was a mistake to keep in touch. But she'd loved him so much that even after that she'd gone on writing—just postcards now and then, and a letter on the anniversary of the day they'd met and the time they'd gone to Vermont, but he hadn't answered any of them, even when she'd written to tell him that her divorce had gone through and she was free at last.

Her impatience made the highway into London stretch endlessly, even though Olivia was fascinated by all she saw. The fields gave way to terraces of small houses and then the larger buildings of the city that still went on for miles until they reached central London.

'Your first visit to London, is it, miss?' the driver asked her.

'Yes. My first to London. My first to England.'

Catching the enthusiasm in her voice, he started pointing out famous landmarks to her, but he needn't have bothered; Olivia recognised them all.

She'd booked a room in a hotel near Hyde Park and the sun was beginning to go down as the taxi pulled up outside. She was hungry and needed a shower, but as soon as Olivia was in her room she made for the phone book. Vaux; it was such an unusual name that there couldn't be many in the book. A smile came into her eyes as she remembered the first time she'd met Nick and he'd introduced himself. 'Nicholas Vaux. Spelt V-A-U-X,' he'd told her with one of his lazy grins, his dark eyes smiling into hers.

Her hands had stilled as she remembered, but Olivia quickly bent to read the book, her finger running down the column. But there was no Vaux, N. And no one at all by the name of Vaux at Nick's address. Olivia frowned, taken aback; she'd been so sure that she would just be able to pick up the phone and call him. Instead she picked it up and called the hotel operator.

'Hi. I'm trying to locate a friend. I have his name and address but it isn't in the book.'

'Perhaps it's ex-directory. If you'll give me the details, madam, I'll make enquiries and call you back,' the polite female English voice informed her.

'OK. Thanks.'

Olivia began to unpack and had hung up her clothes and set up her computer before the phone rang.

'I'm sorry, madam,' the operator told her, 'but there is definitely no Nicholas Vaux listed at the address you gave. But I looked in an old book and he was listed there, so it seems that your friend must have moved out of the London area within the last eighteen months.'

'Gone away?' Olivia said it faintly, unable to believe it. 'But he—he can't have.'

'Perhaps he's listed outside London,' the operator said sympathetically. 'If you like, I could go through all our other directories to try to find someone of that name. I'm afraid it might take quite a while, though.'

'Would you do that? That would be great. Thanks, I appreciate it.'

'No trouble, madam. I'll call you back in a couple of hours.'

Her first elation dampened by the set-back, Olivia took a shower, then went down to eat in the hotel restaurant, making sure she was back in her room well before time. She sat down at the table where she'd plugged in her computer-cum-word processor and tried to put down her first impressions of England, but her mind was too anxious to write anything except that the telephone operators were incredibly helpful. But even so she was pacing the floor and saying, 'Come on, come on,' as soon as the two hours were up.

But it was almost twenty minutes later before the phone finally rang. 'Sorry it took so long; there were a lot of books to go through,' the operator apologised. 'Do you have a pencil and paper?'

But Olivia wedged the receiver against her ear and typed the list of numbers directly on to the word processor as the operator read them out. There were about forty numbers, scattered across the whole of the British Isles. 'Thanks, you've done a great job.'

'If you don't have any luck with these, you could try going to the old address to ask if your friend left a forwarding address.'

'A good idea. Thanks. And thanks for all your help.'

'My pleasure, madam. Just dial nine for an outside line.'

As a journalist, Olivia was used to using the phone to get information, but tonight her senses quickened every time her call was answered, hoping that it would be the well-remembered deep tones of Nick's voice. When it wasn't she would say, 'Hi, I'm sorry to bother you but I'm trying to trace Nicholas Vaux. Do you happen to know him?' Once she thought she was on his trail and her hopes soared, but it turned out to be another Nicholas Vaux entirely, a boy of only seventeen who sounded quite disappointed when he was brought to the phone and Olivia apologised for her mistake.

Her first real clue came when a man with what Olivia thought of as an upper-crust accent said that he had a distant relative by the name of Nicholas Vaux.

'Is he a pilot?' Olivia asked excitedly. 'Did he used to live in London? In his thirties, tall, with dark hair?'

'Could be.' But the voice sounded wary. 'Are you an—er—friend of his?'

'Yes, that's right. We met in the States. I have his London address but he seems to have moved on from there. Do you know where he is now?'

The voice became slightly more friendly. 'Not sure. My wife deals with that kind of thing, and she's away at the moment. Probably taken her address book with her. Hold on, I'll have a look.'

There was quite a long delay before the man came back and said, 'No, sorry, can't help you at the moment. I seem to remember that he went into business. Something to do with helicopters, I think.'

'Can you remember where?'

There was a silence in which she could imagine the man's brain working, and she could almost see him shaking his head as he said, 'Sorry, no. My wife would probably remember. She's good at that kind of thing.'

'When will she be back?'

'Not for a fortnight, I'm afraid.'

'A fortnight? Oh—you mean two weeks.'

'Yes, that's right. Sorry I can't be more helpful.'

'No, you've helped a lot. Thanks.'

Putting down the phone, Olivia sighed with disappointment, then circled the number she'd just called and went on to the next one. A lot of the numbers didn't answer until she'd called two or three times, some not at all, and at ten-thirty she gave up for that day, jet lag catching up with her and making her yawn.

The traffic noise outside was quieter than back home, but the air was still split with the occasional police or ambulance siren on its way to some emergency. Olivia lay in bed but, contrarily, was unable to sleep. She tried not to think of Nick, tried instead to think of the series of articles that she had been commissioned to write by a leading monthly magazine group. Articles which she had really pushed so that she would have an excuse to come over to England—and to look up Nick. Which brought her round full circle. Olivia smiled at her lack of mental control and let her mind go where it would, so that she soon fell asleep with the smile still lingering on her lips.

Next morning, Olivia ate breakfast in her room and tried the numbers she hadn't been able to reach the night before, managed to reach a few but still didn't get any further clues to Nick's whereabouts. He seemed to have just disappeared. Unless his new number wasn't listed yet, or was ex-directory, as the operator had put it. At eleven she realised that she'd been in London for eighteen hours and hadn't even been outside yet. Pulling on a coat and boots, and putting a wide-brimmed, stetson-style hat over her thick, shoulder-length dark hair, Olivia went out into the bright March day.

Trying to remember that the traffic was coming from the wrong direction, she crossed over Park Lane and went into Hyde Park. The trees were bare but there were plenty of people out enjoying the sunshine, although there weren't as many activities going on as she was used to seeing in Central Park. There was a map of London at the entrance to the park; Olivia stopped to look at it, and found Nick's street, his old street, off to the west in an area called Kensington. Looking closer she saw that Kensington Palace was close by. Well, one of the articles she had to write was about the stately homes of England, so why not start at the top?

According to the map it was possible to walk through the park to Kensington from Marble Arch, where she was standing. Olivia set off along Rotten Row, walking at a brisk, long-legged pace, her eyes feasting on everything around her. She passed the piece of water called the Serpentine—no way could you call anything that small a lake, then made her way across to the more sheltered paths of Kensington Gardens. The Albert Memorial, and the Albert Hall directly opposite, held her attention for almost ten minutes but then she turned to go quickly on. When she reached the Palace Olivia stood outside it for a couple of minutes then admitted to herself that she hadn't come to see it at all, and headed instead for Nick's old address.

She found his flat in an Edwardian apartment building in a quiet side-street lined with parked cars. Olivia pressed the bell and a woman's voice told her to come up. The woman turned out to be friendly, middle-aged, and helpful. When Olivia asked if Nick had left a forwarding address she said, 'I don't think we have it, but I'm sure the agents we leased the flat through would know. I'll give you their address, shall I? It's not far away. Just down Kensington High Street.'

Olivia would have liked a look at the apartment where Nick had lived, but the woman didn't ask her in, and she set off again to find the agency, which, as the woman had said, was only five minutes' walk away. By now it was lunchtime and there was only a teenage girl on duty at the agency. Olivia had no difficulty at all in persuading the girl to hand over Nick's new address. Her hand trembled a little as she took the slip of paper but Olivia managed to keep her tone casual as she thanked the girl and left. Outside she eagerly read the address but was immediately deflated as she saw that it was only that of a solicitor in a place called Gloucester, in another place called Glos.

Olivia had heard of Gloucester before but had no clear idea where it was, so she headed for the nearest bookshop and bought an armful of guide books that she carried back to her hotel. Gloucester she found quite easily—it was near the border with Wales—but it took a phone call to the friendly operator to find out that Glos was short for Gloucestershire, which you pronounced Glosstersheer, all one word. Olivia rang the solicitor but got the reply she'd expected—'I'm sorry, we're not allowed to give the addresses of our clients, but if you would like to write to Mr Vaux at this address we will pass on your letter.' And just what good would that do when he hadn't answered any of her other letters? she thought gloomily.

Olivia declined to leave her name and got back to the hotel operator. 'Could you do me another favour? This friend I'm trying to find; there's a possibility that he might be living somewhere near Gloucester, and it's also possible that he could have gone into the helicopter business. I'm not exactly sure in what line of helicopter business, but do you think you—?'

'Could look up all the relevant numbers in that area,' the operator finished for her, sounding amused. 'I'll phone you back as soon as I can.'

Her stomach was making noises so Olivia ordered a meal from Room Service and tried to settle down to do some work while she waited. The articles she had been commissioned to write were on various aspects of Shakespeare's England, and also on the English National Trust, the charitable body that preserved stately homes and parts of the countryside and coastline for posterity. She had acquired quite a lot of information which she'd fed into the computer before she'd left the States, of course, and had prepared a loose schedule of the places she wanted to visit. Now she compared her list with the guide books, and was pleased to find that Gloucester was only about thirty miles from Stratford-upon-Avon.

Her meal arrived and Olivia began to eat, reworking her schedule at the same time, but hastily dropped her fork when the phone rang.

'I have some numbers for you, madam.'

'OK. Shoot.'

'There aren't many, I'm afraid, although there may be other helicopter companies in the area that operate from airports.'

'Well, I'll try these first and get back to you if I don't have any luck.'

There were six numbers. Too eager to eat, Olivia dialled the first one and decided to take a more direct approach. 'I have a message for Mr Vaux; is he there, please?'

There was the usual no, except for one man who said brusquely, 'You've got the wrong company,' and put the phone down on her. Her hopes dying, Olivia tried the last number.

'Evesham Helicopter Services.'

'Is Mr Vaux there, please?'

'I'm sorry, he's out this afternoon. Can I take a message? Hello? Are you there?'

'Yes. Yes, I...' Olivia took a deep breath and pulled herself together. 'I have got the name right—it is Nicholas Vaux?'

'Yes, that's right. Do you want him to call you back?'

'No, that's OK. I—I'll write. Could you give me your exact address, please?'

'It's Harnbury Hall Estate, Harnbury-on-the-Wold, Gloucestershire.'

'Thank you.' Olivia smiled, enchanted by the name. 'And—er—just what services do you offer?'

'We hire out helicopters for all purposes and we also give lessons to trainee pilots. Would you like me to send you a brochure?'

Olivia would have loved one but she said, 'No, that's not necessary. Thanks for your help.'

'Shall I tell Mr Vaux you called?'

'No, it wasn't important,' Olivia replied, and put down the phone. Then sat back and realised what a lie she'd just told. Nick had become the most important thing in her life almost from the first moment she'd met him at a concert in New York, when he'd been sitting beside her and had fallen happily asleep on her shoulder. Her eyes grew dreamy for a few minutes but then she burst into action. Another phone call, to Reception this time, asking them to arrange a hire car for her, to book her into a hotel in Stratford-upon-Avon, and to get her bill ready. 'Oh, and could you arrange for a big box of chocolates to be sent to your telephone operator, please? With my thanks. And tell her I found him. She'll understand.'

The man from the car hire company, seduced by her slim figure and good looks, worked out the route to Stratford for her and sat beside her for a couple of miles until she got the hang of the car and driving on the wrong side of the road in the heavy London traffic. But the other drivers were so courteous and well-behaved that there was really no problem. Olivia could remember driving experiences in some foreign countries that still gave her nightmares.

Once out of London the going was easy; you just got on the wide highways—motorways, they called them in England—until it was time to turn off. 'Stratford-upon-Avon.' The sign came up, and Olivia felt a big thrill as she turned off the motorway. She had always loved Shakespeare, and especially since she had taken the part of Portia in *The Merchant of Venice* at high school. But it was almost dark as she drove into the town and she was too busy concentrating on finding her hotel to look around her very much.

The drive had tired her, and it was too late to try to find Nick today—his company would probably have closed more than an hour ago. Olivia had a meal at the hotel, then took a stroll round the town, but all there was to see were the lighted windows of shops—souvenirs and antiques mainly, so she went back to her room for an early night. But again it was difficult to sleep. She was too excited, too anxious. Would Nick be pleased to see her—or would he be angry? The worst thing would be if he just didn't care. it had been nearly two years since they'd split up, since she'd seen him. Often, lying awake at night like this, she had been tortured by the thought that he might have met someone else, might even be married by now.

Her own life had been such a mess—that too impetuous marriage to Scott Landers when she'd been only nineteen and had fallen heavily for his blond handsomeness, his popularity, and the fact that he had chosen her from all the other girls. Then had come the early realisation that it had been only infatuation, that she'd mistaken first love for the real thing. But the real thing hadn't come along, and she'd tried hard to make the marriage work, but had become more and more caught up with her journalistic career. Scott had resented this and been jealous of her success; *he* had to be the suc-

cessful one, the prize in their relationship, she the ador-
ing consort. Olivia had tried to give him the constant
boost to his ego that he needed until he had started to
demand that she give up her work. This had led to a lot
of fights, but he'd belittled her achievements once too
often and she had finally told him to go to hell and had
walked out.

Scott had sulked for a while, expecting her to come
running back, but when she hadn't there had been a nasty
few months when he had tried to persuade her to go back
to him, playing on her sympathy, making promises that
she knew he wouldn't keep. But he was too late; by that
time Olivia had had a taste of freedom and found it a
heady wine. She had given herself up to her career, made
new friends, a new life. Taken off her wedding-ring, and
even stopped using Scott's name and reverted to her own
name of Grant. In time she went out with other men, but
neither had nor wanted any more emotional ties. Once
was enough. And when Scott cut up rough about a divorce Olivia just let it go hang, not caring either way. For
almost two years she had been perfectly content—until
she went alone one night to a concert and the man in the
next seat fell asleep on her shoulder...

OLIVIA WAS UP EARLY the next morning, trying to disguise with make-up the dark circles round her eyes that
a couple of sleepless nights had left, angry with herself
for looking haggard on the one day when she wanted to
look her best. But the brightness of her eyes, the excited
expectation in them, made up for any lines of tiredness.
She was one of the first down to breakfast, and was soon
in the car, following the route that the receptionist had
marked out for her on a local map. It was another sunny
day, more like early summer than March, the sun low and

bright in the sky so that she had to drive with the visor down, the trees that lined the road casting shuttering flashes of light and shade through the side-window so that at times it was difficult to see.

There was little traffic about and it took less than half an hour to drive the eight miles or so of twisting road to Harnbury-on-the-Wold. It was a small village of old honey-stone houses with lichen-covered tiles on the roofs. There was a church with its door standing open and a woman on her knees outside scrubbing the stone step. There was a little grocery store with bow-fronted windows and a discreet 'Post Office' sign; that, too, was open, and a man came out with a newspaper under his arm, unhitched a dog from a convenient railing and set off at a brisk walk. Olivia smiled; the shop looked like something out of a child's story-book, and she longed to go inside, but right now she had other things on her mind.

Her eyes searching eagerly, she slowed right down, looking for a signboard, but she had driven right through the village and was beginning to think that she had missed it when, half a mile further on, she came to a gateway between high brick pillars with stone balls on top. And on the left hand pillar what she was looking for—a sign which read, 'Evesham Helicopter Services'. And below it a smaller sign: 'Harnbury Hall next left', and an arrow pointing further on down the road.

Pulling into the kerb in the shade of an overhanging tree, Olivia switched off the engine, her heart thumping. She tried to still it, told herself that she was behaving like a love-sick teenager all over again. But she was no teenager now, and knew that this love for Nick was definitely the real thing, the 'now and forever' kind that transformed your whole life. It had certainly transformed hers. She had begun to think of herself as a career girl, devoted to her work, and on the whole content to be so. Admittedly there were times when biology reared its head, making her feel frustrated and lonely, but hard work, that great panacea of all ills, usually cured it. And if that failed there was always a holiday, or self-indulgent trips to the theatre, ballet or a concert.

And it was on one of her concert nights that she had met Nick. Normally she would have gone with a friend, a fellow music-lover, but the friend was unwell and couldn't come. They were playing Grieg, Olivia remembered. She had taken her place, the empty seat beside her, and two empty seats on the other side. They had stayed empty as she read her programme and the concert hall filled. Then, just as the lights went down, a man had come into the row from the other end and sat down beside her. She had given him a quick glance but her eyes hadn't adjusted to the dark and she didn't look at him again. But he was a broad man; she could feel his shoulder against her own. The orchestra began to play and she had forgotten him, lost in the beauty of the music; automatically moving away a little as he had slid down in his seat. And then she had been startled to feel his head against her shoulder and hear his even breathing as he had fallen asleep.

Her first feeling had been of anger, and she had tried to draw away, but his head had moved with her. But then she had become amused and thought, What the heck? The poor man must be awfully tired. So she let him be and gave her attention back to the music. Then the piece came to an end and everyone clapped. Olivia used her elbow to dig her neighbour firmly in the ribs. He gave a little start and woke up. Turning her head, she found herself looking into a pair of surprised eyes in a leanly handsome face. He straightened up, gave an apologetic smile, and sat back in his seat.

Olivia half expected him to fall asleep again but he managed to stay awake and, when the lights went up for the interval, turned to give her another grin.

'Sorry about that. Afraid the time difference caught up with me.' His accent was English, polished, his voice deep and attractive. 'Hope I didn't spoil the music for you?'

She shook her head, her lips curled in amusement. 'No, you snore very quietly.'

'Good lord! Did I? I'm terribly—' But then he saw the laughter in her hazel eyes and broke off to grin again. 'Then you must let me buy you a drink as an apology.'

Olivia hesitated; she wasn't in the habit of responding to a casual pick-up. But that grin *was* attractive, and the circumstances were certainly unusual. But instead of answering she glanced past him to the seat on his other side, which was still empty.

Following her eyes, he gave a sigh of mock tragedy. 'She stood me up,' he admitted.

'Because of your well-known habit of falling asleep during the concert?' Olivia couldn't resist saying teasingly.

The man laughed aloud, making several people look in their direction. 'Something like that. Will you be more merciful?'

She looked at him, taking in his thick dark hair, straight brows over long-lashed brown eyes, high cheekbones and firm, square-jawed chin. His lips quirked a little as she scrutinised him. 'Will I pass?'

Almost to her own surprise, Olivia smiled and nodded and let him escort her out to the bar. He found an empty table for two and dealt quickly and efficiently with getting the drinks. 'I should have arrived in New York this morning,' he told her. 'But my plane was delayed for hours because of bad weather in England. I was supposed to collect my date at her flat but there wasn't time. I rang her but there was no answer so I hoped that she'd done the sensible thing and come here.'

'But she hadn't, obviously.'

'No. Must have given me up as a bad job.' But he didn't sound at all unhappy about it.

'It's a long way to come for a date,' Olivia remarked.

He laughed again, looking her over and liking what he saw. 'My name's Nicholas Vaux. Spelt V-A-U-X,' he told her, his dark eyes smiling into hers.

'I'm Olivia Grant.'

'A beautiful name.' Olivia expected him to make some trite remark about it being a beautiful name for a beautiful person, but instead he sat back and said, 'There was a vacant seat next to you as well.'

'Yes, my friend is sick and couldn't make it.'

'Boyfriend?'

'Girlfriend.'

He looked pleased. 'I suppose you live in New York?'

'Yes.'

'And you love music?'

'Yes.'

He looked pained. 'Have I to guess everything about you? All right, then: I think you're about twenty-two, a college graduate—' his eyes flicked to her left hand '—unmarried, therefore a career girl. How am I doing?'

'Pretty good.'

He looked at her contemplatively. 'Not in the fashion or modelling business—your nails are too short. So perhaps you work some sort of keyboard inst—' He broke off to give an exclamation of triumph. 'Of course! You're a pianist taking a busman's holiday. Listening to the opposition. Am I right?'

Olivia laughed delightedly. 'You were getting warm but went off on the wrong tangent. I do work with a keyboard, but it's on a computer. I'm a journalist. I work for a national magazine company.'

'That's even more interesting. Tell me what you do. Is it for a women's magazine?'

'No, I do features for various journals in the group. It covers a pretty wide range.'

'Do you do investigative journalism—or is that confined to newspapers?'

'Sometimes, when I'm lucky. But all journalists love to do that kind of work, of course.' Almost without realising it, Olivia found herself telling him all about her career ambitions, her fine-boned face becoming beautiful as it lit up with animated enthusiasm.

All too soon the bell was ringing and the audience began to move back into the auditorium. They finished their drinks and Olivia got reluctantly to her feet and led the way back to their seats.

'If I fall asleep again give me another poke in the ribs,' Nick instructed her.

'You must have been terribly tired; couldn't you sleep on the plane?'

His mouth curved. 'Bit difficult when you're flying it,' he remarked, leaving her momentarily stunned with surprise and then having to stifle her laughter as the music began.

During the second half of the performance Olivia was unable to concentrate so much on the music. She was very aware of Nick beside her. It wasn't often that she felt an immediate rapport with anyone, especially a man. Maybe because she had become wary of men since her disastrous marriage. But Nick's attractiveness came over strongly; he was good-looking, charming, and, most unusual of all, he was able to make her laugh. A small stirring of excitement deep inside her took her by surprise. It was a long time since she had felt desire.

What would happen when the concert was over? she wondered. Would he want to see her again and ask for her telephone number? Maybe he might even want to take her home. Olivia didn't like the latter idea, and knew she would refuse; she didn't know him well enough to trust herself to him so casually. She thought of the empty seat beside him and wondered about his date. The girl could be his steady girlfriend or even his fiancée. Whatever, she must have been crazy to stand him up, Olivia decided. Nick didn't try to take her hand or anything, just sat quietly now, listening to the music. But once, almost as if he was aware that she was thinking about him, he turned his head and smiled, his eyes holding hers.

Something inside Olivia's chest gave a jolt and her eyes widened as she gave a small gasp, then quickly turned away and sat back in her seat, her emotions chaotic. For a while she was too stunned to sort her feelings, then felt a great rush of gratitude, followed almost immediately by one of indignation. She had been so careful to keep her emotions under control and not get involved with anyone, and now here they were pitching her willy-nilly headlong into a new relationship. That she and Nick would become involved, would have a relationship, Olivia was somehow absolutely sure. And with that certainty came a sudden feeling of intense excitement and anticipation.

The concert came to an end, the music finishing on a great crescendo of sound that was only slightly louder than the thumping of Olivia's heart. She joined in the applause, glad to have something to do with her hands, but had to stop when the conductor took his last bow and the players started to leave the stage. She picked up her bag and moved with the rest of the audience out of the hall, Nick following her. When they got outside she turned to him. 'Thanks for the drink.'

'Where would you like to have supper?'

'What about your date?'

Nick smiled at her. 'I'm beginning to think she did me a great favour.'

'Well, I don't know...' Olivia prevaricated.

'I promise not to fall asleep again,' he urged.

She laughed. 'OK—but only on that condition.'

Lifting his arm, Nick hailed a cab. 'Do you like Italian food?' And when she nodded he directed the cabbie to a good Italian restaurant that she'd heard about but hadn't yet tried.

'You obviously know your way around New York,' she remarked.

'Mm, I've been on this route for almost five years.'

'You're a commercial pilot?'

'For my sins.'

'Are you based in England or New York?'

'England. London. I fly out of Heathrow.'

'Which city do you prefer?'

He gave her a lazy grin and stretched his arm along the back of the seat. 'Ah, I think this is where I have to be careful. Are you dreadfully partisan?'

'Dreadfully—I have to be; I've never been to London.'

'In that case I shall say that I love New York when I'm here and I love London when I'm there.'

'Coward,' she mocked. 'But London is home?'

He nodded. 'Yes, I suppose so.'

They reached the restaurant and were shown immediately to a table. It was just crowded and just noisy enough to give the place a good atmosphere. There were red cloths on the tables, Olivia remembered, and candles stuck in Chianti bottles that were encrusted with the wax of a hundred earlier candles. For ten minutes or so, while they looked at the menu, they discussed food and wine, their likes and dislikes. When the waiter came Nick gave their order in Italian.

'Do you speak many languages?' Olivia asked.

'You tend to pick up a smattering of wherever you fly to. Enough to get by when it comes to food and drink, anyway.'

'Ah, so you get your priorities right.'

Nick laughed and reached out to lightly touch her hand. 'I'm glad I met you.'

Nick was in New York for three days and they saw each other every day, spending the whole of Sunday together. They talked a lot, learning about each other, but somehow Olivia couldn't bring herself to tell him about her marriage. She had the feeling that this new, as yet fragile relationship was too precious to spoil by talking about a past she wanted to forget. And they didn't go to bed together, not that time or on his next couple of lay-overs. But on the day he was due into New York about a month later he phoned her at her apartment just as she was about to leave for work.

The line was faint, with some static. 'Where are you?' she asked, raising her voice.

'Halfway across the Atlantic. Listen, I've persuaded the powers that be to let me have a week's leave in the States. How about persuading your boss to let you have the time off, too? Maybe we could take a holiday somewhere.'

Olivia's breath caught in her throat and it was a few seconds before she could say, 'No strings?'

Nick laughed softly. 'Lots of strings.'

'I'll have to think about that.'

'I'm due in at eleven-thirty your time. Why don't you meet me at the airport at noon? That will give you time to pack a bag.'

'Hey! I said I'd have to think about it.'

'Just think about where you'd like to go.'

He rang off and Olivia sat looking at the phone, her mouth gradually breaking into a big smile, her face soft.

They went to Vermont, staying in a log cabin in the Green mountains, used by skiers in the winter but surrounded now with heavy-foliaged trees and wild flowers that carpeted the ground. Olivia had expected to be nervous, but Nick made everything easy and wonderful, so that going to bed with him felt right and natural. He made all her sensual feelings come alive again, made her feel as if her emotions had been hibernating, lying dormant and afraid to emerge, but now blossoming out with spring and summer all rolled into one. Engulfing her, lifting her to dizzying heights of excitement that she had never known.

When the week was over neither of them wanted to leave. On their last night they lay in front of a log fire and Nick held her close, occasionally kissing her lightly as they listened to music from the portable CD player—Vivaldi this time. Pushing himself up on his elbow, Nick looked down at her, his eyes tender, smiling. 'I shall remember this week, and treasure the memory always,' he told her huskily.

'I'm glad it's been good for you. For me it's been—' she gave a small laugh to hide the depth of her feelings '—an amazing experience.'

Nick's eyebrows rose. 'Amazingly good or amazingly awful?'

'Amazingly *wow*!' Sitting up, she put her hands on either side of his face. 'But I didn't have to tell you that. You know how you made me feel.' Olivia chuckled. 'The whole mountain moved.'

'I'm glad.' Nick kissed her lightly. 'We must do it more often.'

'You can say that again,' she answered, in such heartfelt tones that he laughed.

His left eyebrow rose. 'How about now?'

'I thought you'd never ask.' And, for Olivia, Vivaldi had never before finished on such a climax.

From then on, whenever Nick had a lay-over in New York he came to stay in her apartment, giving that term a whole new meaning. Olivia gave him a key, letting him enter her home as he had entered her life.

For two months her happiness was perfect. Too perfect. Something had to go wrong, and it happened when she got home from work one evening and found Nick waiting in the apartment for her. She knew he would be there, was expecting him, and rushed eagerly to greet him, throwing her arms around his neck and laughing, smiling, talking all at the same time, her face ablaze with happiness at seeing him again. But then the laughter died as he stood still, making no attempt to respond.

'What is it? What's happened?' she demanded in sudden fright.

Tersely, he said, 'There was a phone call while you were out. I thought it was you so I answered.' Nick's mouth and eyes grew bleak. 'It was a man. His name was Scott Landers—he said he was your husband.'

He watched her keenly, waiting for her reaction. A bitter taste came into Olivia's mouth, and anger that her happiness had been intruded upon from the past. 'My marriage was over two years ago.'

'You're divorced?'

For a moment Olivia was tempted to lie, but she knew that Scott would have told Nick that they were still married, that he would have enjoyed pumping poison into her new relationship. So she shook her head. 'No, he made all sorts of difficulties so I just let it go. I thought he might change, given time, and I wasn't in any hurry to marry again.'

'It seemed it wasn't a very amicable parting?'

Olivia gave a rather bitter laugh. 'Can separation ever be entirely amicable? I left him, and he didn't like it. If anyone was going to walk out he wanted it to be him. So he lied and told everyone that he kicked me out.'

Nick made an impatient gesture. 'Does it matter?'

Her head came up. 'No, it doesn't matter now, not to me. As far as I'm concerned it was all over a couple of years ago, except for a piece of paper making it official.' She paused, then said with difficulty, 'Nothing's changed, Nick.'

'Except that it didn't occur to you to tell me that you had a husband somewhere around.'

'He's part of my past I want to forget about. I didn't want it to—intrude on us, on our relationship.' She spoke persuasively, trying to take the withdrawn look from his face, the anger from his eyes.

But Nick's voice was cold as he said, 'So just when did you propose to tell me—if ever?'

'I don't know.' She shrugged helplessly. 'When the time was right, I suppose.' She saw his lips thin at that and caught hold of his sleeve. 'Nick, please try to understand. I'd put the whole thing behind me, was trying to forget it. And when I met you I didn't want anything to spoil what we have.'

'And if I'd asked you to marry me?'

Her breath caught. 'Then naturally I would have told you; you would have had the right to know.'

'I see.' But he still seemed angry. 'So it would have taken complete commitment on my part before you would have bothered to tell me that you just happen to have been married and hadn't got round to getting a divorce.'

His attack made her feel guilty so she attacked in return. 'So what difference does it make? You haven't asked me to marry you. And if you—if you love me you won't care about my being married before.'

'I thought you were free,' Nick retorted curtly. 'I believed what you told me—that you had never been in love before.'

'But I *haven't*!' Olivia said desperately. 'Not like this. What I felt for Scott was only infatuation, a teenage crush that I mistook for love. It was a mistake that ruined years of my life. But I knew almost from the first moment I met you that this was for real. And you felt it too; I know you did.'

'What I feel hardly seems to matter,' Nick said shortly. Turning, he picked up his uniform hat and his flight-bag. 'I don't break up marriages, Olivia.' And he started for the door.

Filled with dreadful fear, she ran to stop him. 'No, you can't leave. Not like this. Doesn't what we have mean anything to you?'

Nick gazed at her, his face bleak, his jaw grim. 'That's what you don't understand. It means *everything* to me.' He gave a grim smile at her stunned face and opened the door. 'When—or should I say *if* you ever do get a divorce, let me know; I may still be free myself.' And he walked out, firmly closing the door behind him.

THE SUN REFLECTED off the windscreen of a car coming towards her, catching Olivia's eyes, blinding her. She put up a hand to shade them and saw the car turn into the open gateway. For a brief instant she caught a glimpse of the driver's profile, and her heart gave an unforgettable, achingly longed for jolt. She had found Nick at last. After a few minutes Olivia reached out to start the engine and followed him through the gates.

CHAPTER TWO

ONCE through the gates, Olivia had expected to come immediately upon helicopters and hangars, but the way ran through a long avenue of tall trees, their bare branches black fingers against the blue sky. A fork in the road and another sign with an arrow pointing off to the right. Olivia followed it as the land rose quite steeply, then she emerged from the trees on to open ground, a large plateau of land looking out across a valley, beautiful even in winter. The hangars were here, and several helicopters standing ready for take-off, their white paintwork gleaming in the sun. There was also a single-storeyed office building with a few cars parked in front of it, one of them the car she had seen Nick driving. She parked to one side, out of line of the office windows, and walked slowly towards the building, her heart thumping in her chest. Anxious, eager, terrified, full of the aching yearning that had brought her this far, Olivia went up to the door and pushed it open.

The first thing she heard was Nick's voice talking to someone, coming from an office down a corridor that led off the reception area. She had loved his voice so much, and once every tone had been a caress. For a moment Olivia had to shut her eyes and dig her nails into her palms before she could go on. She started to cross the room but a woman in her late thirties came out of a door to the left and said, 'Good morning. Can I help you?'

Olivia quickly shook her head and put a finger to her lips. 'No. I—I want to surprise Nick.'

The woman raised her eyebrows, hesitated, but let Olivia go on down the corridor alone. Nick's office was at the far end, the door open. He was talking on the phone, his feet up on the desk, sitting in a swivel chair with his back to her, reading through a letter as he talked. Olivia paused in the doorway, trying to still her chaotic emotions, her hand gripping the door-jamb, glad of these few moments when he didn't know she was there.

The room was very neat, very businesslike; filing cabinets lined one wall and the only items of decoration were photographs and souvenir parts of old biplanes on the far wall: a compass, control column, and brightly polished propeller blade. Nick's voice stopped suddenly, and she saw his shoulders grow tense. He wasn't looking at the letter any more; his head was raised, his eyes fastened on the mirror-like surface of the propeller blade. Following his eyes, Olivia saw her own distorted reflection.

For a long moment he didn't move, just sat as if frozen, then he said into the phone, 'Look, I'm sorry, but something's come up; I'll have to call you back.' Putting the receiver down, Nick swung his legs off the desk and swivelled round in the chair to face her.

His face was very pale, stunned. Olivia looked eagerly into it, searching for the love they'd known. For a few moments his eyes seemed to drink her in avidly, but then his jaw tightened and he blinked and looked away. She waited for him to speak, but when he didn't said softly, unsteadily, 'Hello, Nick.'

'Olivia. This is—quite a surprise.' His fingers were gripping the edge of the desk but his face was taut now, almost wary.

She had hoped for a much warmer welcome than this; Nick didn't even stand up and come to greet her. He was behaving almost as if they had been nothing more to each other than casual acquaintances. The thrill of anticipation turning to overwhelming disappointment, Olivia slowly stepped forward into the room, pushing the door shut behind her but standing near it, almost as if she needed its support. Her eyes were still on his face, noticing lines around his eyes and mouth that hadn't been there two years ago. He looked older, world-weary. She wanted to take him in her arms and smooth the lines away, but his churlish welcome stabbed at her pride. Her head came up and she tried to hide the hurt behind light casualness as she said, 'I guess it must be. But I thought I'd look you up as I was in your neck of the woods.'

'Really?' He put his hands under the desk, then shoved them in his pockets. 'How did you know I was based here?'

But Olivia already had the answer to that one prepared. 'I met another British Airways pilot at a party in New York, someone who knew you; he told me where you were. So, as I was due to come to England, I decided to see how you were getting along.'

Nick had been watching her keenly but she had managed to keep her voice light and casual and he seemed to relax a fraction. 'Just fine, as you can see.' He glanced at his watch and somehow Olivia managed to hide the bitter hurt the gesture caused. 'Look, I've got to pick up a customer in twenty minutes or so, but I'm sure we have time for a coffee. Why don't you pull up a chair and tell me all that you've been doing? I expect you're famous over in the States by now?'

Before she could answer he picked up the internal phone. 'Jane, bring in a couple of cups of coffee, will you? Quick as you can.'

Slowly Olivia walked over to a chair a few feet away from his desk and sat down, propping her bag on the floor beside her but making no attempt to move the chair nearer. His facetious question had angered her and she found his lack of manners in getting the chair for her himself humiliating. 'No, I'm not famous,' she said coldly. 'I don't suppose I ever will be, but I'm still working as a journalist, if that's what you mean.'

His eyes flicked to her face at her tone, then immediately away again. 'And are you over here on holiday?'

Trying to match his detached casualness, she replied, 'No, I'm working on a series of articles for the magazine company.'

'You must be successful, then. Congratulations.'

There was a silence, a tense, difficult few seconds until Olivia said, 'How about you? What made you give up flying the big jets?'

'Oh, I just got tired of the life. Decided to have a go at being my own boss.'

'And are you successful?'

There was a brief knock on the door and Jane came in with two cups of coffee on a tray. She put the tray on Nick's desk and went to leave, but he said, 'Serve it for us, would you?'

'Of course.' The woman looked at Olivia. 'Do you take milk and sugar?'

'No, just as it comes. Thanks.' She took the proffered cup and watched as the woman added a little milk to Nick's, obviously used to his taste. Jane left and Olivia looked down at her cup as she stirred it, fighting back the raw hurt of rejection.

Picking up her last question, Nick said, 'The business is gradually expanding. I have five helicopters now.'

'You're not the only pilot, then?'

'No, there are three of us full time, and two part-timers who mainly give flying lessons.'

Olivia lifted her cup to her lips but didn't drink, her throat too tight to swallow. Desperately she sought for something to say and could only come up with the trite, 'Is it difficult to learn to fly a chopper?'

'No, quite easy once you get the hang of it.'

Another taut silence in which Olivia put her cup down on a small table beside her. 'So you're settled in England now?'

'Yes.' He said it firmly, with a curt nod.

'And married, presumably?' The question burned her throat, made her lips dry.

Nick visibly hesitated before saying tersely, 'No. And you?'

'I got my divorce.' Slowly, painfully, she added, 'I wrote and told you but you didn't answer my letter.'

'Did you? Perhaps it went to my old address. I moved some time ago.' His eyes went to his watch. 'Look, I'm sorry to rush you but the mornings are always busy and—'

Olivia got hurriedly to her feet. 'Sure, I understand. Nice seeing you again.'

'And you. You won't mind seeing yourself out, will you? I must finish that phone call before I leave.'

She nodded and walked blindly out of the office and down the corridor, desperate to get away and be alone. She felt for her car keys in her pocket and almost ran through the empty reception area and out to the car. Getting in, she automatically started the engine to drive away, unable to think straight, her mind full of choking unhappiness. She started to drive down the road from the office building, but she couldn't concentrate, and her hands were shaking too much. When she reached the fork Olivia realised that there was no way she could safely drive out on the main road, so she swung the wheel and took the turning leading away from the entrance, and when she came to a convenient place pulled off the narrow road and parked the car behind a huge rhododendron bush, out of sight of anyone who might pass.

For several minutes Olivia sat quite still, her eyes closed, going back over the long-anticipated meeting with Nick which had turned out to be so disastrous. It had all gone so hopelessly wrong. He had been shocked to see her, yes, but then, what man wouldn't have been surprised to see an old flame, an ex-lover that he had almost forgotten walk back into his life? And he had soon let her see that she wasn't welcome, that he was no longer interested.

Not for the first time, Olivia wondered if finding out about her marriage had been a convenient excuse for Nick to end their affair, that he'd been cooling off anyway. And yet she'd been so sure that he still loved her, had noticed nothing to give her any indication that he was tiring of her. Back then she would have been willing to bet every cent she possessed that he was still as hot for her as ever, if not more. And during that first and last row he'd even mentioned marriage, so how could he have changed so completely? OK, it had been almost two years. Two years in which she had at first been sure that he would relent and come back to her. She'd gone to a lawyer about a divorce at once, but Scott had gone to work abroad and blocked her at every turn so that it had taken over a year before the divorce had finally come through. Maybe Nick had thought that she hadn't really cared about him, that she hadn't been doing all she could to hurry it along, even though she'd written to tell him of her difficulties.

Olivia suddenly hit the steering-wheel with her clenched fist. How could he have been so cruel to her when they had been so close, had meant so much to each other? He could at least have been kind; he must have realised that she wouldn't have looked him up unless she still cared, still wanted him. Tears came to her eyes as she remembered the long empty nights and days after he'd gone away. There hadn't been one day since that she hadn't missed him unbearably, hadn't longed to be with him again. It was like the loneliness of grief, but made worse because she had the torment of knowing that if only she'd told him about her marriage at the start they might still be together.

And it would have been so easy, she could see that now. When Nick had looked at her ringless hand and said 'Unmarried?' she could have just said, 'Not quite. I'm separated, about to be divorced.' Why hadn't she, for heaven's sake? Olivia cursed herself yet again for not doing so. And now it was too late. Nick had been embarrassed to see her, and given her a shoulder so cold it had frozen her heart.

Suddenly she hated him, loathed him. OK, so he didn't want her, had more than likely found someone else by now if that hesitation when she'd asked him if he was married meant anything. So to hell with him. At least she could stop hoping against hope that everything would be OK again once they saw each other. It had been a stupid, idiotic hope anyway. In her heart she had always known that too much time had passed, that if he'd loved her he would have come back to her long before this. She'd just been a lovesick fool, clinging to a memory, a

useless, forlorn dream. Abysmally stupid enough to waste
another two years of her life over a man. Well, not again,
never! From now on she was on her own and was going
to stay that way for the rest of her life. And she might as
well start right now! Olivia reached for a handkerchief to
blow her nose but her bag wasn't on the seat beside her.
She looked in the back, searched round on the floor, and
then remembered with horror that she must have left it in
Nick's office.

Oh, hell! Olivia would have dearly loved to abandon
the bag rather than go back, but it contained her pass-
port and all her money. She hit the wheel again, furious
with herself, biting her lip, knowing she had no choice but
to go back. Then she remembered that Nick had said that
he had to collect a customer shortly; he must surely have
gone by now, and she seemed to remember the sound of
a helicopter engine. Relaxing in a flood of relief, Olivia
leaned her head against the side-window for a few moments, then wiped her eyes with her fingers and got out
of the car. The ground rose steeply to her right to where
the level plateau and the helicopter hangars must be.
Rather than go back along the lane, Olivia walked up
through the trees, picking her way through a white sheet
of snowdrops and the thick buds of daffodils. Primroses
sheltered in the grassy banks, and beneath a great copper beech just coming into bud there was a long swath of
winter aconites, their yellow petals as golden as the sun.

She came out of the wood almost opposite the last of
the hangars and walked round its edge until she reached
the car park. Wiping her eyes again, she walked, chin
high, into the building, intending to ask Jane to get her
bag for her, but the reception area was empty. Olivia
hesitated, but then was glad; now she could just go and
collect it herself without anyone seeing her. She walked

quickly and quietly down the corridor to Nick's office, but came to a hasty, frozen stop in the open doorway. Nick hadn't left; he was still there, sitting with his elbows on the desk, his face buried in his hands, his shoulders sagging in dejection. Olivia stared open-mouthed, completely taken aback, anger turning to incomprehension. Nick gave a small sound, almost like a deep, agonised groan, and she quickly backed away from the door and tiptoed silently back down the corridor.

In the reception area she leaned against the counter, groping through her chaotic emotions, trying desperately to understand. There was a bell on the counter to summon attention and she accidentally put her elbow on it. Jane came into the room. 'Leaving already?' she asked with a smile, obviously not knowing that Olivia had left before.

Trying to hide her consternation, Olivia said, 'Yes, I— I'd like a brochure.' Jane handed her one and, summoning her wits, Olivia pretended to notice the absence of her bag. 'Oh, my purse! I must have left it in Nick's office. Would you mind getting it for me, please?'

'Yes, of course.' The woman looked surprised, but went to do as she asked. Olivia heard her speak to Nick, and a moment later she came back with the bag. She gave Olivia an odd look as she held it out. 'Here you are.'

'Thanks. Bye.'

Hastily dropping the brochure in her bag, Olivia walked dazedly away from the building again. Glancing towards the choppers, she saw that one was missing, but whoever had flown it away it wasn't Nick. Had he lied, then, to shorten that dreadful meeting? He had been so determined to let her see that she was an unwelcome intrusion from his past and that he couldn't wait to get rid of her. Maybe too determined. Olivia's thoughts raced as wildly as her heart. Had Nick's real emotions showed when he'd been alone, had thought her gone? When he'd looked so terribly unhappy?

But why? Why, if he'd still felt something for her had he hidden it, and hidden it so successfully behind an abruptness that was close to being downright rude? Coming to the trees again, Olivia walked on for a few yards then stopped and leaned against a tree-trunk, not knowing what to do, what to think. Her heart filled with the wild hope that for some unknown reason he still loved her but didn't want her to know. And more than that he had been determined to antagonise her so much that she would keep well away from him in future. But that was crazy, impossible. Trying to think it through logically, using her trained observer's mind, the only other reason for Nick's behaviour that Olivia could come up with was that he must be feeling unwell. He had certainly looked very pale at first, but she had put that down to seeing her so suddenly. Olivia gave a mirthless laugh of self-mockery; maybe she was kidding herself that he still felt something for her when all the time he was just nursing an almighty hangover!

Not knowing what to think, she went to turn and go back to the car, but as she did so heard the main door of the building open and then close. Moving behind the thick trunk of a tree, where she could see but not be seen, Olivia saw that Nick had come out. He stood there for a moment, zipping up a black leather jacket he had changed into, and looked up at the sky, studying the formation of the clouds, a typical pilot's gesture. Then he began to walk across to one of the waiting helicopters. Only he didn't exactly walk. Instead he limped, not badly, just favouring his right leg, the long, energetic stride that she remembered completely gone.

Olivia drew in her breath, realising now why he hadn't moved from his chair. Something had happened to him, something terrible—and he hadn't wanted her to know! The unexpectedness of it held her riveted for a long moment, but he was coming nearer and she whirled round and ran back through the trees and down the slope, careless of the wild flowers, making sure that he didn't see her. When she reached the car Olivia leaned against it, out of breath, a flame of colour in her cheeks. Her heart was thumping, but not from running; it was singing with renewed hope and joy. The crazy fool! The stupid, wonderful, crazy fool! Olivia got in the car and tears ran down her cheeks again, but from relief this time. He must have been hurt in an accident of some kind. For a moment her mind froze with horror as she imagined him being hurt so badly, being in pain. Why hadn't he sent for her? She would have given up everything to be with him, surely he knew that? But she pushed the thought aside; it was too late to think of that now—it was only the future that mattered. If she was right, if Nick had put up this wall of stubborn pride around himself, then she had to think of some way to break it down.

Olivia didn't know what had happened to Nick's body, but she was as sure as hell going to make sure that he started thinking straight again, and the sooner he admitted that he still loved her, the better!

CHAPTER THREE

THE sound of the helicopter's engines shattered the stillness of the morning. Looking up through the car windscreen, Olivia caught a glimpse of it flying north. 'Fly safely, my love,' she murmured. 'Oh, please take care.'

The lane was too narrow to turn the car; Olivia had to reverse to the fork before she could turn and head back to the main road. She had made no plans for the rest of the morning, had been unable to think past meeting Nick, and now she was glad she hadn't because there was no way she could concentrate on any work today. For half an hour or so she just drove around aimlessly, but presently came to a small town busy with traffic. Feeling unable to cope with it and longing for a coffee, Olivia followed the 'P' signs to a car park, and gratefully abandoned the car. The town, Bourton-on-the-Water, was obviously a tourist resort in summer, and even now cars lined the main road and there were visitors walking around, admiring the old Cotswold stone buildings and the shallow river that ran parallel to the road with pretty little stone bridges crossing it.

Olivia found a bow-windowed coffee-shop and dived inside to sit at a table near the window, where the sun shone through like a solarium. She drank two cups of coffee without a pause and, feeling a little better, sat back in her chair to think. If she was right—oh, God, please let me be right, she prayed—and Nick still cared for her, then it looked as if she had a difficult situation on her hands. Difficult, but not impossible. As long as she handled the whole thing with tact and delicacy; sledgehammer tactics were definitely out of place when it came to a man's pride. Again she wondered anxiously what had happened to Nick. The most likely thing was a car accident.

A thought occurred to her, and Olivia grew still; was that why she hadn't heard from him for months and then he'd written to end it all? Her heart tightened in her chest. Oh, she hoped so, she certainly hoped so. It explained so much that she hadn't been able to understand. That letter had been the biggest confidence-killer she'd ever known—far worse than the realisation that she had made a mistaken marriage, because it had hit not only her pride but her heart, too. It would have broken her if she'd been able to accept Nick's cold words, but somehow she had always clung to the hope that it was a mistake. And she could never bring herself to believe that he could be that cruel, that ruthless.

Feeling better, Olivia paid for her coffee and went for a walk alongside the little river. There were grey and white ducks swimming through the water; they looked cold, their feathers fluffed out. On impulse Olivia went into a bakery and bought a loaf of bread still warm from the oven, then found an empty wooden bench near the river's edge and threw some crusts into the water. It was as if a message had travelled the length of the river; soon she was surrounded by ducks jostling one another for the bread, quite tame and unafraid. She tried to be fair, throwing some out to the ducks that had been pushed to the back, but soon the loaf was all gone, although the ducks stayed. 'Sorry, fellas, you've had the lot.' She stood

up and brushed the last crumbs from her skirt into the
water, then turned to walk on.

She had to think of some way of seeing Nick again;
until she did there was no way she was going to start to
break down that barrier. But how, when he had been so
cold and dismissive? Come on, brain, get to work, she
told herself. Look on Nick as someone you want to in-
terview but won't let you near him. Now, where is he
most vulnerable? Of course, the helicopter business.
Finding another seat, Olivia searched in her large travel-
bag and pulled out the brochure. Reading it through
carefully, she came to the conclusion that she would either have to hire a chopper or learn to fly one. But she
remembered Nick saying he had two part-time pilots who
did the teaching, so it looked as if it came down to hiring
one. Olivia grew dejected again, realising that even if she
did Nick would make sure he didn't fly her himself. But
there had to be a way round it, there just had to be.

She got restlessly to her feet again and decided to go
back to the car. Taking a last look round the town, she
realised what an attractive place it was, despite the cars.
It would have been better to have seen it a hundred years
ago, maybe even two hundred, when it was just a sleepy
little town and tourists had never even heard of it, but it
still managed to be beautiful.

It took quite a while to find her way back to Stratford,
following signposts with arms two yards long to accom-
modate names like Stow-on-the-Wold and Lower and
Upper Slaughter. Having eventually got back to her hotel, Olivia thought she'd better do some work, and got
out her guide books, but her mind wouldn't settle. She
took out the brochure again and sat staring at it, then a
small smile came to her lips. It was worth a try. If she
could carry it off. If she could afford it. Olivia looked

again at the scale of charges on the brochure; it was going to be expensive, but luckily her grandmother had left her quite a lot of money only the year before, and as the old lady had been romantically minded Olivia was quite sure her grandma would approve of her legacy being spent in this way.

Going down to Reception, Olivia gave the man on duty her best smile. 'Could you do something for me, please?'

He blinked and grew a couple of inches. 'Certainly, madam. Anything at all.'

'I'd like you to make a phone call for me. To this number.'

'But you can call from your room. The phone system is quite easy.'

'Yes, I know, but I don't want to make the call myself.'

Carefully she explained what she wanted him to do, and he repeated, 'I'm to say I'm making the booking on behalf of a travel company who want to hire a helicopter three days a week for the next four weeks. And to insist that the helicopter be piloted by the proprietor Mr Nicholas Vaux. What if they ask me why?' he queried.

'Say that the travel company's operative is nervous of flying and insists on having an experienced pilot. Don't let them fob you off with anyone else. If they do, say the deal's off. And don't say my name at all and keep the gender neutral.' He raised his eyebrows. 'Don't tell them I'm a woman, just keep saying operative or representative. And be careful not to say she,' Olivia amplified. 'Ask them to have a contract all drawn up ready to sign. Have you got all that? It's vitally important you get it right.'

'Yes, madam.' The man gave her a disparaging glance and shrugged, his opinion that all Americans were crazy confirmed for all time. But he picked up the phone and dialled the number. Olivia watched and listened eagerly, terrified he would make a mistake, her clenched fists on the desk as she willed him to get it right. He was magnificent, not slipping up once, and within minutes he had confirmed that Nick would definitely be available to fly her, starting the day after tomorrow.

Olivia could have hugged him. 'That's fantastic. You British hotel staff are just *great*!' She almost danced back to her room and threw herself down on her bed, rolling on it in joy. Then she lay and gazed up at the ceiling, a big smile on her face. Aloud she said, 'Nicholas Vaux, you don't stand a chance.'

That afternoon she worked, if exploring one of the oldest and most beautiful towns in England could be called working. As excited as she was about Nick, Olivia was soon lost in awestruck wonder at the wood and plaster houses, their upper floors projecting out over the street, that were to be found in almost every street of the town. She went into Shakespeare's birthplace, and felt like crying at the wonder of being there. She trod the old sloping floorboards that creaked beneath her feet, gazed at the room where the great man was born, and spent a long time poring over the exhibits in the tiny museum in one of the upper rooms. Afterwards she went out into the garden at the back of the house and walked along a path between scalloped beds of thyme and basil and sweet marjoram. Looking back at the house, Olivia could almost see Mary Arden, Shakespeare's mother, coming out to pick herbs to add to the evening meal. The sense of history was so overwhelming that she almost forgot to record her reactions into her hand-held microcassette recorder. Olivia looked at the gadget and chuckled: a jump of four centuries in as many seconds.

The next day Olivia spent visiting all the places in Stratford that had American connections, like the beautiful half-timbered house in the High Street which was once the home of Katherine Rogers, mother of John Harvard, the founder of Harvard University. Then there was the American fountain in the market-place, and the window donated by Americans in the church where Shakespeare and his family were buried. And she also went into the Teddy Bear Museum because she couldn't resist it. In the evening she wrote up her notes on the word processor, trying to concentrate, trying not to let her mind ceaselessly think ahead to tomorrow.

At nine-thirty the next morning Olivia drove again to Harnbury-on-the-Wold and through the gateway that led to the heliport. She was wearing a thick sweater, jeans and boots, and had brought with her a jacket in case it was cold, sun-specs against the bright morning light, and a flight-bag containing her cameras and guide books. She wanted to appear as professional as possible even though her heart was fluttering with nervous tension. If anything, she was more nervous today than she had been two days ago; so much depended on her ability to carry this through, to more or less force Nick into keeping his promise to be her pilot.

When she drove up to the buildings, Olivia went straight into the office and signed the contract that Jane had waiting for her, filling in all the necessary details and making sure it specified that Nick would act as her pilot. It took a while, and when she came out she saw Nick standing in the distance beside one of the helicopters, his back to her, talking to a white-overalled mechanic. Quickly she went over to where she'd parked the car in the shade of the office buildings, collected her things from the back seat and locked it. Then said a last but forceful prayer. She was already wearing the sunglasses, and kept them on as she took a deep breath and turned to go across to Nick—and found him walking towards her.

'Good morning,' he called out. The sun was in his eyes and he put a hand up to shield them. 'Are you from the travel company? Afraid I don't know—' He stopped abruptly as she came nearer. 'Olivia!'

'Hi. It's a great morning, isn't it? I can't wait to get started. Are we all set to go?'

She walked past him towards the waiting chopper, but he reached out and grabbed her arm. 'What the hell are you doing here?' he demanded tersely, his fingers digging into her.

'Hey, that hurts.'

But he didn't let go. 'Is it you who's hired me to fly them around? Is it?' he repeated forcefully.

'Why, sure. But you knew that; didn't your secretary tell you?'

'No, she damn well didn't, because you made sure not to give your name.'

'Well, I was busy so I didn't make the booking myself; I asked someone at the hotel to do it. Did they forget to give my name?'

Nick's face hardened. 'They said it was for a travel company.'

'Oh, really, these hotel staff—you can't trust them to do anything,' Olivia lied indignantly. 'I said it was for a travel *feature*.'

'Did you really? I wonder why I don't believe you.'

Olivia didn't even blush. 'What does it matter? Are we all set to go?'

'*We're* not going anywhere. Did you really think that you could get away with this ploy? Do you think I don't see through it?'

'What do you mean?'

The direct question took him by surprise. Nick's eyebrows drew into a frown and he let go of her arm. His jaw tightened and he said shortly, 'There's nothing between us any longer, Olivia. It's over. Finished. I stopped feeling anything for you long ago.'

It was cruel and it was meant to be. But Olivia had expected nothing less and didn't even flinch. She laughed, again taking him completely by surprise. 'Well, I already knew that. You made it plain enough last time. And if we'd had time to talk I would have told you what a relief it was to hear it. Mind you, our—er—affair was great while it lasted and I wouldn't have missed those months for worlds. Matter of fact, I still feel pretty nostalgic about that time—that's one of the reasons why I looked you up. But then I realised you might get the wrong idea and think I wanted to pick up again, so I was pleased when you made it clear you didn't.'

'Really?' Nick still looked totally disbelieving. 'What were the other reasons?'

'For looking you up? The fact that you were based in this area and that you had the chopper business, of course.' He was still frowning so she let a patient note come into her voice and said, 'I'm doing a series of travel features on the Cotswolds, stately homes, the National Trust, Shakespeare's England, that kind of thing. I decided to base myself in Stratford-upon-Avon because it's near the Cotswolds and because it's so central. But I only have a limited time and I wanted to get round to see as much as possible, so I needed to hire a chopper to beat the traffic jams. So I thought as you were an old friend I would put the business your way. We are still *friends*, aren't we?' she added, thankful for the dark glasses.

He ducked that one, the coward, instead saying, 'Why didn't you tell me any of this before?'

'There was hardly time. And I must admit I was a little nervous about seeing you again in case you got the wrong idea. But it was so long ago; it hadn't occurred to me until the last minute that you might take my visit to mean that I was still interested. But luckily you didn't,' she said with a sunny smile.

'No.' Nick's eyes were on her face, studying her, but he couldn't ask her to take off the glasses because Olivia had been careful to move round so that she was facing the sun. 'Why didn't you tell me you wanted to hire one of my choppers?'

But she had the answer to that one, too. 'I hadn't seen your brochure; I didn't know whether my expenses would cover your hire charges.'

The simple reply took him aback. He gave a little negative shake of his head, as if he didn't know whether to believe her or not, but then his head came up again as he said, 'But why insist on having me as your pilot? All of my staff are fully qualified and competent.'

'I expect they are, but I *know* you're good. And was it you or someone else who told me always to insist on the best?' She laughed again and indicated the cameras in her open flight-bag. 'Besides, you're more likely to be patient with me when I ask you to fly around in circles while I take photographs.'

Nick's eyes narrowed. 'I didn't know you were into photography.'

'Well, I probably wasn't when I knew you. I took a course on it about eighteen months or so ago, so that I could do photo-journalism. The publishers like that; it saves them money if they can send one person on an assignment instead of two.' She managed to say it casually, not wanting him to guess that she had been so lonely, so desolate when he had left her that she had taken the course to give herself something to do, a challenge to try to take her mind off her unhappiness for a while.

'The other pilots are as good as me if not better,' Nick said firmly. 'We've one due in about an hour. He can take you wherever you want to—'

'No!' Olivia cut in firmly. 'Didn't whoever booked for me tell you? I'm—I'm nervous of flying in a helicopter. I'm not going to trust myself to just anyone. It has to be someone I can trust. And what's the point in waiting round for an hour when you're all ready to go?'

'Olivia, I don't think it would be a good idea for us to—to be cooped up together for hours on end.'

'Why not? I thought you said you'd stopped even thinking about me ages ago.'

'I have.' He came to a stop, his eyes angry and frustrated.

'Well, that's OK, then. After all, if I were anyone else you wouldn't hesitate to take on such good business, would you?' She glanced at her watch and said impatiently, 'We're wasting time. I have a heavy schedule.' And she walked past him to look at the helicopter.

It looked quite small and fragile and altogether too clumsy to fly. Olivia sighed. It was true that she didn't enjoy flying in them—not that she was afraid, they just made her feel queasy; she had been up a couple of times during other assignments, but it was far from being her favourite method of transport. But if she couldn't get close to Nick any other way, then this had to be it.

He came up behind her. 'Where do you want to go? I'll have to get the maps from the office and work out a flight plan.'

Olivia closed her eyes in a paean of gratitude. She had won; he was going to take her. Turning, she immediately became businesslike. Taking her map book from her bag, she opened it at a marked page and said, 'I want to fly the length and breadth of the Cotswolds so that I can take some aerial shots, and this afternoon I want to go to this place.' She pointed with her finger. 'Blenheim Palace, near Oxford.'

'We can't just turn up there,' Nick objected. 'They may not allow helicopters to land.'

'They do; I rang them and checked. It's all fixed; we're expected.'

Nick gave her a baleful look. 'You were very sure, then, that I would do as you wanted.'

She gave him a surprised look. 'Why shouldn't you?'

His lips thinned but Nick only said, 'I'll go and get the maps.'

She nodded and looked away as he limped back to the office building. Reaction set in, and Olivia began to tremble. She would have dearly loved to sit down and close her eyes, but as there was only the ground to sit on she reached up and took off her glasses and put up a hand to her head.

'You all right, miss?'

Hurriedly opening her eyes, Olivia saw that the mechanic had come round from behind the chopper and was looking at her curiously. 'Oh, sure. Fine. The sun's so bright today.' She gave him a smile and put the glasses back on. 'Hi, I'm Olivia Grant.'

'Bill Fairford.' She held out her hand to him, but he laughed and shook his head, then showed her his oil-soaked hands. Evidently he had been told to expect a nervous customer because he came to stand beside her and looked almost lovingly up at the chopper. 'No need to be afraid,' he told her. 'You'll love it when you get up there. And Mr Vaux's a real good pilot; you can have every confidence in him.'

It occurred to Olivia that here was her source of information, but it was too soon to take advantage of it; Nick might ask Bill if she'd questioned him, so she just said, 'Oh, yes, I'm sure he is. It's just that it seems such an unnatural way to fly. And it upsets my stomach when they drop so suddenly.'

'That's just bad flying,' Bill said earnestly. 'You won't have to worry about that with Nick. Bet you a quid you enjoy yourself.'

'Well, I'm always willing to take a bet, but what's a quid?'

Bill gave a guffaw of amusement. 'A quid's a pound. One of these.' He fished a coin from his pocket and showed it to her. 'I'll collect it from you when you get back later.'

'I hope you do,' Olivia answered truthfully.

'Hope he does what?' Nick had come up to join them.

'Just telling the lady that she's nothing to be afraid of,' Bill explained hurriedly, but he winked at Olivia before he turned away.

'Let's get your gear inside.' Nick picked up her bag, limped over to the chopper, opened the door and put it inside.

She followed and handed him her jacket. Nick tossed it in then looked into her face as if he was waiting for her to say something. For a second she didn't understand, then realised that he expected her to have noticed his limp and to make some comment about it. Lifting her leg, she put a foot on the skid and reached up to pull herself into the helicopter, saying lightly as she did so, 'What have you done to your leg—pulled a muscle?'

It gave him an out if he wanted to take advantage of it, and he had a few moments to decide as he walked round to the other side and climbed in. When he was sitting beside her she gave an enquiring glance. 'Something like that,' he said shortly.

He turned away to close the door and Olivia bit her lip in chagrin, but then chided herself for being silly. What other answer could she possibly have expected? After the way he'd tried to get rid of her Nick was hardly likely to just turn round and confide everything at the first opportunity. No, it was going to take a lot more time building up his trust before they would become close enough for that.

Nick showed her how to do up her strap, gave her a head-set to put on, and showed her how to use it. 'All set?'

Olivia nodded and, remembering she was supposed to be nervous, gripped the edges of her seat tightly.

His face skeptical, Nick said, 'You never used to be nervous of flying.'

'A jumbo jet is a slightly different proposition from a two-seater chopper,' Olivia retorted.

'But you weren't afraid when I borrowed that two-seater plane to fly us to Vermon—' He broke off and turned abruptly away, but it was too late; that one word had conjured up memories that Olivia could only hope would still be as vivid for him as they were for her. And at the least it proved that he hadn't forgotten completely.

The knowledge that he still remembered thrilled and
excited her, gave her hope, but his slip had angered Nick.
'Ready?' he demanded shortly.

'I guess so. I just hope I don't feel air-sick.'

Nick gave a short, mirthless laugh. 'You're about to
find out.' He started the conversation-killing engine, the
rotors began to turn, and within minutes the chopper
lifted off the ground.

CHAPTER FOUR

FOR all his inner anger Nick flew the helicopter smoothly, without any dips or sudden sideways swoops. As the ground receded, Olivia's thoughts were mainly on her own frailty and even more on the machine's, but after the first few minutes she relaxed enough to let go of the seat and look out.

'Which direction are you going?' she asked into the microphone in front of her mouth.

'South.' The answer came back tinnily through the headphones. 'Do you want towns, villages, or open countryside?'

'All three. But I have to be careful not to get our shadow in the shot.'

He nodded, evidently having done it all before. 'There's a mount fitted to the fuselage that you can attach your camera to.' He reached his gloved hand across to point. Olivia leaned forward to see, and he immediately moved his arm so that he didn't touch her.

Taking her camera from the bag, Olivia was glad enough to turn her back on him as she concentrated on fitting it into position.

'We're over Chipping Campden now,' he told her.

'Oh, what a beautiful church.' She looked down in delight at the Gothic windows and pinnacled tower. 'How old is it?'

Nick hesitated, as if he didn't want to talk, but said reluctantly, 'It's one of the great wool churches.'

Putting a hand up to press the headphones nearer to her ear, Olivia said, 'Did you say wood?'

'No—wool. The area grew rich on sheep in the Middle Ages and the merchants gave money to have the churches built or enlarged.' He pointed over to some fields where the white dots of sheep stood out against the green. 'See those sheep? Their ancestors probably go back in this area as far as man's.'

Olivia liked the idea. She smiled and got him to fly round a couple of times to get the right angle for her photographs. They flew on, and she asked Nick more questions, using him as a guide, and so breaking through his taciturnity whether he liked it or not. It felt strange and yet wholly right to be with him again, to have his shoulder and occasionally his knee brush hers, to feel that thrill of excitement invade her heart, her body. But it was important that he didn't suspect her thoughts, so Olivia kept the questions professional but used his name a lot, reminding him that she was more than just a customer. She treated him as an old friend, and made it plain that she expected him to treat her in the same way. At first he was guarded, withdrawn, and her determined casualness beat like light upon his persistent gloom, but after a couple of hours he was talking to her almost normally, even volunteering information.

Being casual towards him was made easier because she spent so much time looking out for good shots—and seeing far too many of them. Olivia was enchanted by the softly rolling countryside, the sleepy, timeless villages, by all she saw. The early spring sunshine lay across the fields and turned the meandering rivers into molten silver. 'Oh, look!' she exclaimed with delight at a meadow golden with daffodils. 'How beautiful. I must get a shot of that.'

To her amazement she heard Nick give a crack of laughter. She turned to him, eyebrows raised. 'You sound like the proverbial American tourist,' he told her.

She laughed in return. 'Bad as that, huh?'

His eyes settled on her face, vivacious and alight with amusement, then flicked away. His voice abrupt again, he said, 'We'll have to make for Blenheim soon, if you want to get there in time.'

'Already? But surely we haven't covered half the Cotswolds yet?'

'Not even a quarter—you've taken too many photographs.'

Olivia smiled. 'I could never take enough shots.' But she sat back as Nick swung the helicopter towards the east.

She had been so busy taking photographs that she had forgotten her fear of queasiness, and now she found that, not only was she perfectly comfortable, but she was also enjoying herself as Nick climbed higher and increased the speed. I owe Bill Fairford a quid, she thought, and smiled to herself. Glancing at Nick, she caught him watching her, a frown of curiosity in his eyes. She remembered that look from when they had been together, when they had been lovers. Then he would have asked her what she was thinking about, what was so amusing; he would have wanted to share her thoughts, for her to have no secrets from him, as no part of her body was secret from him. But today he looked away, stifling his curiosity, fighting any personal remark, any contact that would bring them even fractionally closer.

A few miles from Blenheim Nick dropped down to a small airfield to refuel. Olivia got out to stretch her legs and bought a couple of Cokes and two brown bread rolls bursting with cheese and lettuce and tomato. Walking away from the petrol haze and smell, she found a bench in the sun and sat down to wait for Nick to join her.

He did so reluctantly, impatiently. 'We're ready to go on.'

'Sit down, have a drink first.' She held out one of the cans. 'I'm thirsty, aren't you?'

'We'll be late.' He stayed standing, frowning again.

Olivia glanced at her watch and said, 'Plenty of time for a lunch-break. Here, I got you a roll. You do like cheese, don't you? I'm afraid I can't remember.'

Slowly he sat down beside her and took the roll. 'Thanks.'

'You seem to know a lot about the Cotswolds,' Olivia remarked. 'Have you learnt so much in eighteen months?'

'Eighteen months?'

'Since you started the chopper company,' she explained.

'Oh, that.' Nick hesitated. 'No, I used to live round this area when I was a boy, and I've often been back here for holidays.'

'It must be a wonderful place to live. Where do you live now? In Gloucester?'

He gave her a quick look. 'What gave you that idea?'

From finding out that was where his solicitors were based, but Nick, of course, wasn't supposed to know that. Cursing the mistake, Olivia said lightly, 'That's the nearest big town in the area, isn't it? I don't see you living anywhere that doesn't have a theatre or—' she gave him a look under her eyelashes, wondering how he would take it '—a concert hall for you to fall asleep in.'

He had been watching her closely, but the memory had thrown him off the scent as she had hoped it would. In the brief moment that he let his eyes meet hers, Olivia read in them pain and a kind of consternation. Then he turned away, but she so wanted to know, was so desperate for reassurance that she couldn't leave it alone, and said, 'Have you fallen asleep on many shoulders since I last saw you?'

Nick took a long drink of the Coke, his throat muscles working, then he crushed the empty can in his hand and tossed it neatly into a litter-bin. 'It's not something I'm in the habit of doing,' he answered curtly. He stood up. 'I'll be at the chopper when you're ready.'

Olivia watched him go, feeling as though he had given her a mental slap in the face. It hurt as much, the way he'd said it, as if it was a mistake he didn't care to repeat. Slow down, she told herself. You're going too fast and putting him on the defensive. How the hell do you expect him to react when you ask such a leading question?

Unhurriedly, Olivia finished her roll and Coke and strolled over to the chopper. Nick was looking at a map and hardly glanced at her as she climbed in. As soon as she was strapped in and the headphones on he took off and didn't speak to her again until they reached Blenheim and she relayed the instructions she'd been given on where to land. They flew over the house first, and she gasped at the size of it.

'I've seen pictures of this place,' she said in excitement, 'but nothing could prepare you for the real thing. How many people live there?'

'I think only the Duke and Duchess of Marlborough now—and their staff, of course.'

'All that for two people,' Olivia said wonderingly.

'Given by a grateful nation to the first Duke for saving us from the French,' Nick said flippantly, but there was admiration in his eyes, too.

'And where your Winston Churchill was born.'

'They'll show you the very bed in the very room.'

She looked at him quickly; if they hadn't been so far apart she would almost have said that he was teasing her, but he was looking out through the side window as they came in to land and she couldn't see whether there was amusement in his eyes or sarcasm.

There was no time to dwell on it. As soon as they'd landed a man came forward to meet her. 'Miss Grant? I've been designated to act as your guide. Welcome to Blenheim Palace.' He turned to Nick. 'Your 'copter will be quite safe here if you'd like to get yourself some refreshments in the café.'

Olivia collected her gear and followed the guide, a little amused that Nick had been treated as nothing more than her chauffeur. But that was what he was, she supposed—a far cry from being the captain of a jumbo jet and responsible for four hundred passengers instead of one. It worried her, and she knew that she wouldn't rest until she'd found out why—no, until Nick told her why himself. But right now she had to put it out of her mind and concentrate on her guide and Blenheim. Which was no hardship at all; the house was so beautiful that it was impossible to think of anything else, even Nick.

It took over three hours to go over the house and some of the gardens, and Olivia could easily have spent longer, but she had promised Nick to be back at the chopper by five so that they could get back before dark. She sincerely thanked her more than helpful guide, and ran back to where Nick waited, the setting sun reflecting off the windows, making the chopper look as if it was on fire, engulfing Nick as he leaned against it, waiting.

She arrived breathlessly, her hair flying about her head, her hazel eyes dancing with laughter. 'I feel like Cinderella,' she gasped. 'I was afraid that any moment you might change into a pumpkin and a mouse.'

He didn't speak, and she supposed that he'd found the remark childish and silly, but when she looked into Nick's face Olivia found his eyes fixed on her, wide and vulnerable, as if he couldn't tear himself away. She wanted to throw herself in his arms then, to tell him that she loved him, wanted him, needed him. To tell him that it didn't matter, whatever had kept him away from her, that she was here now and that everything would be all right, all right! She tried to tell him so with her eyes, opened her mouth to say it with her lips, but at that moment a cloud drifted in front of the sun, plunging them into gloom. Nick blinked and glanced up. 'We'd better get going. It's clouding over.'

They hardly spoke on the way back. The sun disappeared completely behind clouds and they ran into a shower of rain as they covered the last few miles. Olivia didn't mind; she felt completely safe, completely content shut away here with Nick. And she felt a great surge of optimism; just this one day had proved beyond all doubt that he was by no means immune to her, however much he tried to pretend otherwise. And she had four whole weeks to work on him. Olivia's heart was lighter than it had been since the day he left her. She wanted to laugh and shout and sing, but instead she concentrated on taking her camera from the mount and stowing it carefully away in her bag. When they landed back at Harnbury she turned to Nick. 'Thanks a lot; it's been a very successful day. I'll go and see Jane to settle up with her.'

'She's probably gone by now; see her next time.'

His voice was unemotional but the very fact that he was willing to contemplate another time added to Olivia's happiness.

'OK. See you in a couple of days.' She lifted her hand in farewell and jumped out of the chopper, but instead of making for her car ran over to the hangar, where she could see Bill Fairford sheltering from the rain. She put a coin in his hand. 'I owe you a quid,' she laughed, then sprinted through the rain to her car.

That evening Olivia ate great food in a great atmosphere at Fatty Arbuckle's restaurant in the town, went back to the hotel intending to work, but felt so tired that she went straight to bed and slept better than she had in weeks, waking up the next morning feeling great. After breakfast she booked a ticket for that evening's performance at the theatre built on the edge of the River Avon, and then took a trip on the open-topped bus that toured the town, braving the breeze to sit on the top deck and see everything from a new angle. The bus went on to pass Anne Hathaway's cottage at Shottery and then Mary Arden's house at Wilmcote, both of them so perfectly picturesque that they looked as if they'd been specially built for a movie. In the afternoon Olivia worked, writing up her impressions and roughing out a couple of articles.

The play that night was *As You Like It*, performed by the Royal Shakespeare Company in the Swan Theatre, built as a replica of the old Globe in London, the round theatre where Shakespeare himself had once acted. Olivia came away enchanted, her mind clinging to what she'd seen, never wanting to forget, her soul still in the Forest of Arden. And that night she dreamt herself back there, but it was Nick who pursued her through the trees and carried her back to a palace that strangely became the log cabin in Vermont.

Olivia's only anxiety the next morning was about the weather, but it was another lovely clear day. She re-loaded all three of her cameras and took a different route to Harnbury, arriving there just on time, not wanting Nick to think her too eager. A chopper was waiting and a man in a leather jacket standing by it. Olivia walked over with a smile, said, 'Hi,' but the smile faded as the man turned round and she saw it wasn't Nick.

'Good morning. You must be Miss Grant.'

'That's right. Where's Nick?'

'He sends his apologies; he's had to go to a business meeting this morning. I'm to take you up today.'

She should have expected this, Olivia realised bitterly. But she had been so busy congratulating herself on how successful she'd been so far that it hadn't occurred to her that Nick would do the dirty on her and duck out. 'When will Nick be back?'

'No idea. Certainly not till after lunch.' He reached forward. 'Let me take your bag for you.'

But she stepped away. 'No, thanks. I guess I'll wait for Nick.'

The pilot, as tall as Nick but about ten years older, gave her a look of male condescension. 'I assure you, you'll be quite safe with me.'

'I prefer to wait for Nick.'

'He said that you'd got over your initial nervousness.'

'It's suddenly come back again,' Olivia retorted, and strode towards the office building.

Jane was talking on the phone; she lifted a hand in greeting when she saw Olivia and mouthed, 'Won't be a minute.'

Olivia nodded, set her flight-bag on a chair and walked down the corridor to Nick's office. She had quite expected to find him there, that he'd lied about going out, but the room was empty. Going over to his desk, she flipped open the engagement diary placed neatly by the telephone. Under that day's date there was an entry: 'Accountant 9.30.' 'Miss Grant 10a.m.', in what must be Jane's writing, had been scored through. Maybe it was a genuine excuse but Olivia didn't think much of it. Nick could easily have arranged to see his accountant some other time.

'Now do you believe me?' The pilot had followed her, and spoke from the doorway.

'Yes, I believe you.' Olivia closed the book and he stood aside to let her pass. 'But I guess I'll wait for Nick anyway.'

'But that's ridiculous. He could be hours. And you've booked a chopper for the whole day so you'll just be wasting your own time and money,' he protested.

Ignoring him, Olivia went up to Jane. 'Would you please ring Nick at his accountant and remind him that he agreed to fly me himself? Tell him that I won't be fobbed off with anyone else and that I'm waiting for him to get back here and carry out his part of our agreement.' She turned to the other pilot with an apologetic smile. 'Sorry.'

He shrugged. 'Suit yourself.' And went through the door on the left of the reception area.

Jane gave Olivia a worried frown. 'I can't disturb Nick when he's with his accountant; he wouldn't like it. And he certainly wouldn't like your message.'

'Too bad,' Olivia replied shortly. 'Here, I'll do it if you're too scared.'

She reached for the phone, but Jane said hastily, 'No. No, that would be even worse. All right, I'll phone him, but don't blame me if he's angry.'

Olivia smiled. 'Thanks. I guess I'll take a walk while I'm waiting. I'll go that way.' She pointed off past the hangars towards the open valley.

'But that's private.'

'Really? Well, if Nick doesn't want me to be arrested for trespassing he'd better get back here fast. Tell him so.'

Turning away, Olivia left Jane to get on with the call, and walked out into the open. At first she was inclined to be angry with Nick and think him a coward. Did he really think she couldn't see through his ploy? If she'd accepted the services of the other pilot this time then Nick would make sure to find other excuses not to fly her himself, and she'd end up with the other pilot every day. But then it occurred to Olivia that she must have had quite an effect on Nick to make him try to duck out this way. The thought pleased her, but then she sighed; she should have known that things were going too well to be true. Now she had another fight on her hands.

The ground fell away quite steeply from the edge of the plateau on which the hangars were built. They were well screened by trees and bushes, but from here she could see down into the valley where the sun coruscated off the rippling waters of what looked like the beginning of a lake off to the left, the rest of it hidden by a thick belt of coniferous trees. Olivia started to walk down the hill, enjoying the sun and the slight breeze that lifted her hair. The sound of birds filled the stillness as they busily gathered materials to make their nests. It must be nice to be a bird, Olivia decided, to fly and soar in that incredibly blue sky, to have no difficulty in grabbing a mate, and insisting on a new house every year.

The thought made her smile. She ran down the last few feet of the hill to a dry stone wall surrounding a meadow full of cowslips, their golden heads hanging like delicate bells that swung in the breeze. Olivia climbed on the wall and balanced on its top for a moment. As she did so, she caught a glimpse of the roof and chimneys of what must be a large house down in the valley, among the trees, but she was much too entranced by the cowslips to take much notice.

Carefully jumping down to a clear space, she began to pick some of those flowers that were fully in bloom, wandering aimlessly down the sloping meadow as she did so. When her hand was full and she couldn't hold any more, Olivia sat down on the grass and looked dreamily around her. It was so beautiful here, so peaceful. She could hardly believe that less than a week ago she'd been part of the New York rat race. A picture of hooting traffic in clogged streets, the smell of gasoline fumes, and jostling, hurrying people filled her mind. She had enjoyed being part of New York, had found the frenetic life a constant challenge, and still did—but, looking out over that perfect landscape, she wondered if she would ever enjoy it quite so much again.

It was almost half an hour later before Nick came. Olivia was lying on the grass, her eyes closed, but she knew he was there even before his shadow blotted out the sun. Without opening her eyes, she said, 'I went to the theatre last night. It was *As You Like It*. I guess Shakespeare called it the Forest of Arden because that was the name of the forest north of Stratford. It doesn't seem to be much of a forest now. Did it used to be much bigger?'

'I wouldn't know. When you've seen one forest you've seen them all,' Nick returned harshly.

Ignoring his anger, Olivia said dreamily, 'Talking of Shakespeare plays, lying on this bank makes me feel like Titania. Do you think Shakespeare ever came here?'

'I doubt it.'

Olivia raised languorous eyelids, looked at him towering over her, and sighed. 'I bet Oberon was a swine to have around, too.'

Despite himself, Nick's lips twitched in amusement, although he quickly hid it behind a frown. He hesitated for a moment and then dropped to sit down beside her. 'I don't go much on being called away from a meeting by a jumped-up women's page contributor who thinks she's God's gift to journalism,' he said curtly.

'Oh, that's not bad,' Olivia said admiringly. 'But somehow I don't feel crushed by it. Have another try.'

His face tightened. 'I have a business to run. I have other commitments besides pandering to your whims, you know.'

'I'm a customer; I'm allowed to have as many whims as I can pay for.' She sat up, pieces of grass clinging to her tumbled hair, and looked into his eyes. 'And right now my wish is to have my old friend Nick Vaux to act as my pilot and guide. Is that too much to ask? For old times' sake?'

For a long moment their gaze met and held, then Nick dragged his eyes away and looked down at the ground. He had obviously expected her to be angry, and had been spoiling for a fight himself—a real humdinger that would have ended their friendship once and for all, and it had thrown him when she refused to rise to the bait. He pulled some long grasses from the turf, squeezed them almost viciously between his fingers. 'Let someone else fly you, Olivia.'

His voice was terse, almost pleading, but Olivia ignored it. 'There looked to be quite a big house over in the valley; is it open to the public?'

'No, it's private.' Nick dropped the pieces of grass and tried to rub the green stain from his hands.

Slowly, feeling her way, Olivia said, 'What we had was very special, Nick. Please don't spoil it.'

'You can't go back,' he said fiercely. 'Everyone knows that. You shouldn't have come here if you didn't want your—your precious memories spoiled.'

His tone hurt, but Olivia said calmly, 'I don't want to go back.'

He turned to her then, his face set and bleak. 'Well, there's no going forward, not with me.'

Somehow she managed to control her feelings and return his look unblinkingly. 'I thought we'd already sorted all that out,' she said as lightly as she could. 'Look, Nick, you're the only person I know in England; why shouldn't I look you up? Have you got a steady relationship going or something? Doesn't your girlfriend approve of your flying me around?'

She waited for his reply, trying desperately to conceal her inner tension. It would have given him an excuse to drop her, but Olivia knew that he would never lie to her, no matter what. And she sighed with inner relief when he shook his head. 'No, it's not that.'

'So what are you afraid of?'

'Afraid?'

He gave a short laugh, so full of bitterness that Olivia's heart was wrung with pity. But he would never want that. She caught her breath and grew still; maybe it was her pity that he was afraid of. Olivia tried to put herself in his position; would she want his pity if she'd been hurt in some way? Definitely not. But she would want and need his strength, his encouragement to get well in mind and body. The thought filled her with a kind of gratitude; at least she had some idea now how to handle things. Without waiting for him to speak, she gathered up her posy of cowslips and rose gracefully to her feet.

'Let's get going, shall we? The morning's almost gone.'

Nick heaved himself up with a lot less grace. 'You're not supposed to pick cowslips,' he told her. 'So many people have done so in the past that they're now a protected species.'

Olivia gazed at him in alarm. 'You're kidding! No, you're not. Well, I can't put them back. What do I do? Do you think the owner of the field is around?' she asked, looking guiltily over her shoulder.

'You can always plead ignorance,' Nick commented, his eyes amused. 'And I expect the owner will spare you those few flowers for the sake of Anglo-American relations.'

'Well, that's a relief.' She glanced at him, thinking that their own Anglo-American relationship could do with some improvement right now. At the same moment Nick looked at her and she knew he was thinking exactly the same thing. Olivia laughed aloud, and after a pause Nick, too, grinned reluctantly. 'So you haven't lost your sense of humour after all,' she remarked. 'I was beginning to wonder.'

But it was the wrong thing to say. Nick immediately tensed up. 'I suppose I seem a lot different to you.'

'Different?' Olivia shrugged. 'Not particularly. Why should you?'

'I should have thought that was obvious,' he said tersely.

They had come to the wall, and she let him help her over it, then turned to face him. 'Your attitude to me is different, of course. But then it would be, I suppose.' She gave him a pert look. 'And I must admit that you seem to be a lot less sexy than I remember.' She laughed at the indignant look he shot her and began to run back up the hill. 'Come on, what are you waiting for? I've got places I want to see.'

After that day Nick didn't again try to get out of flying her—probably because he knew it wouldn't work. The following week they flew over the Cotswolds in the mornings and off to some stately home or other in the afternoon. Over the weekend and on the in-between days Olivia either worked or got out the car and drove to places that were near by—like Warwick Castle, where she spent the whole day lost in medieval times. And with every place she saw she became more enchanted. It was as if her sense of history, dormant since she'd left college, had come vibrantly back to life. She fell in love with each golden-stoned village under its moss-encrusted roofs, with every ancient, musty church that smelt of damp and dust, with the stones in the graveyards whose lettering grew fainter as they receded into time. Enchantment filled her at every daffodil-edged stream, at the first lambs frisking happily in their new world, at the fat, sticky chestnut buds opening into leaf.

Her pleasure in this beauty was given with unstinting joy, perhaps especially so because when Olivia was with Nick she had to be practical and businesslike. Usually when she met him in the mornings she could sense the tension in him, but as the day progressed he gradually relaxed, would become more like the Nick she had known in New York, but never entirely. There was always some part of him that was held in iron reserve, a barrier she couldn't break through, and she began to despair that she ever would.

And she had so little time; it seemed to be racing by. Only very rarely was there even a glimpse into his heart. There had been that first day in his office when she had seen him with his head in his hands, and a couple of times she had turned quickly and caught him watching her, his eyes so bleak and lost that he seemed to be in pain. It took great will-power then to show no sympathy, no love, but somehow Olivia managed it, knowing it was the only way.

Once she even teased him about his limp; they had left the helicopter in a field about three-quarters of a mile from the mansion Olivia had arranged to visit, the nearest place they were allowed to land. The day had become overcast, and they were early so Nick suggested walking to the local pub for a drink and a sandwich. But they had only gone about halfway when the sky darkened completely and there was an unseasonably heavy shower. The swinging sign of the inn—the Goose and Firkin—was in sight, so Olivia ran ahead of Nick and stood waiting for him in the porch. He followed her, walking fast, but when he arrived his hair was plastered to his head and he had to flick it away from his eyes. She gave him a cheeky grin. 'Well, at least the girls won't have any trouble running away from you now.'

A startled, almost bewildered look came into Nick's dark eyes, and for a long second Olivia thought that she'd made a mistake, but then he grinned, and it was a cheerful grin. 'Rubbish—they never run away from me.'

'You hold them by the force of your personality, I suppose?'

'Of course.' He held open the door of the pub for her to go in. 'Come on; maybe they do lunch.'

They did. A variety of pies in earthenware dishes, the pastry top so light that it rose a couple of inches above the dish and flaked like snow when it was cut into. Olivia chose oyster and mushroom filling, and Nick hunter's pie with venison and rabbit and hare. With it Olivia had wine and Nick a pint of real ale, made at a local brewery, the landlord said, thick and dark—and warm, of course. Nick had always said that American beer shouldn't be served so cold.

She smiled at the thought, and Nick said lightly, 'Penny for them.'

The question pleased her, because it proved that he was much more relaxed with her, but she didn't know if the answer would please him; she was always careful not to remind him of their time together. 'I was just thinking that you never really liked cold beer when you were in the States.'

But he didn't seem to mind. 'It was OK in your fryingly hot summers. It would be out of place here.' The meal eaten, he sat back in his seat, at ease, the lines around his mouth not so deep. It was still raining heavily, beating against the window-panes, so no new customers came in. Some left, running to their cars, the few that stayed were all in the other bar. They had been alone together in the helicopter of course, but there was always the noise of the engine and the inhibiting head-sets between them there. Here Olivia felt really alone with him, and it was comfortable sitting in the low bar with its beamed ceiling and wide ingle-nook fireplace, the firelight reflecting off polished copper pans and horse brasses that had been there for a hundred years.

Nick glanced out of the window. 'You'll wait until it stops?'

'Yes.' He had put a hand on his knee and was unthinkingly rubbing it. 'Does your leg ache when it's damp? When I broke my leg skiing one time it ached for years afterwards when it was cold or damp,' Olivia added quickly in case he thought she was asking out of sympathy.

He hesitated a moment, then nodded. 'It's much better than it was.'

'Did you break it?'

'Yes.' He got up and went over to the bar, bought another round of drinks and brought them back to the table. At first he didn't speak, just sat looking down at the thick white froth on his beer, then he said, 'I fractured it in a couple of places, but it's healed well. There's virtually nothing I can't do with it that I did before,' he told her on a defiant note, almost as if she'd challenged him, 'but it's left me with one leg slightly shorter than the other. I suppose I could have it put right, but I've had enough of hospitals.'

There was a depth of pain behind that last sentence that left Olivia in no doubt that there was far more to tell. She said nothing, trying not to imagine the suffering he had gone through and which had left him so crippled physically, and perhaps mentally too.

Nick took a long swig of beer, then said, 'You're being very tactful.'

'Am I?'

'Don't you want to know how I did it?'

'Do you want to tell me?' she countered.

She saw his hand tighten on the glass, but then he shrugged as if he didn't care. 'It was nothing much. I was in an accident.'

'A car smash?' Olivia asked levelly.

His mouth twisting into a mirthless grin, Nick said, 'No, a plane crash.'

At Olivia's gasp of horror he turned to look at her, his eyes wary, ready to be antagonistic. 'Your plane crashed? Oh, my God! When did it happen? I don't remember reading about it in the paper. Were many people killed?' She stared at him, her hands to her mouth, her eyes wide and appalled.

'No,' he said quickly. 'You've got it wrong. I wasn't working when it happened. It wasn't a big jet.' He reached out to touch her arm in a gesture of apology—the first time that he had voluntarily touched her since she'd come to England. 'I wasn't even flying the plane. I was a passenger in a biplane at an air show,' he explained. 'Something went wrong and we crashed.'

'Oh, Nick.' Olivia was unable to keep the deep emotion she was feeling out of her voice, out of her eyes. But she saw Nick's face harden, and she quickly pulled herself together. 'What a terrible thing to happen. But you seem to have recovered very well. You were lucky to get off so lightly.'

Nick gave her a strange look. 'Yes.'

A biplane, he'd said. Olivia remembered the photographs of an old plane in his office and the propeller on the wall. At the time she'd been too full of emotion at meeting Nick again to do more than glance at them, but the plane must obviously have meant a lot to him. Gropingly she said, 'And—and the pilot? Is he OK too?'

'No.' His jaw tightened and he looked away. 'He wasn't so—lucky.'

'Do you mean that he was killed?' Olivia asked painfully when he didn't go on.

'Yes.' Nick swallowed the rest of his beer and stood up. 'The rain doesn't look as if it's going to let up. I'll phone the house and ask them to send a car for you.'

He went to walk past her, but Olivia reached up and caught his hand. 'The pilot—was he a close friend?'

Nick paused, looking down at her, his eyes so bleak and cold that she shivered inside. 'Yes,' he replied, 'I suppose you could call him a close friend. He was my father.'

CHAPTER FIVE

THAT afternoon's stately home was a National Trust property only just opened up to the public again after a winter in dust-covers, so that everything was bright and clean. Olivia was made welcome and given a guide to herself, but the rooms were high and large and there was little heating so it felt very cold. Because of the weather there were few visitors so the guide took her on a very leisurely tour. Olivia tried hard to concentrate and take notes, but her mind kept going back to Nick. After he'd telephoned for a car for her he had virtually ignored her, going over to the bar to chat with the landlord. Maybe he was already regretting having confided about the plane crash. Feeling completely unnerved, Olivia had gone out to the Ladies' and stayed there until she heard the car draw up outside.

'Where will I find you?' she asked Nick, trying to sound matter-of-fact.

'At the chopper if it's fine. Here if it's still raining; the pub stays open all day.'

She'd nodded and left him, unable to find the words there and then—to express her sympathy, to give comfort? Olivia gazed dutifully at a painting of the third Earl and wondered if she'd reacted as Nick had expected, or as he'd wanted. Somehow she didn't think the two were the same. And whatever reaction she'd had it would probably be wrong. The thought left a bitter taste in

Olivia's mouth. But she comforted herself with the knowledge that at least he'd told her.

'And this is the Earl's cousin, Lady Marjorie.' The guide leaned towards her and lowered her voice as if she was imparting a secret. 'As a matter of fact it's thought that she and the Earl had a clandestine affair. At any rate she produced three children out of wedlock and the Earl paid for their education. But then, she was a relative so he would probably have done so anyway, I suppose. Of course she was quite *shunned* by society after that—although it would have been all right if she'd been married, of course.'

Olivia didn't see the logic in that. She gazed up at the face of the Earl's mistress. She was blonde, pale and insipid; but then, most of the women's portraits looked like that, as if the same artist had come and done a job lot. She certainly didn't look as if she had enough nerve to flout society and give up everything for love.

They moved on and Olivia's thought went back to Nick. Could *she* give up everything for him? she wondered. Life had been wonderful while they had been together in New York; she had had the best of both worlds—her work that was good and stimulating, a constant challenge, and Nick to make love to her whenever he was in town. And that side of their relationship had been more than wonderful; it had given her life an emotional meaning that she could have gone on through the years not knowing even existed. He had been a fantastic lover, so virile, so masculinely lustful. Sometimes he'd walked into her apartment and within five minutes they'd be in bed.

And it had been fun, too. Olivia's eyes softened as she remembered the surprises he'd pulled, the way he'd teased her. Once they'd been to see a film where the heroine came home to find her apartment full to the ceiling with balloons, and Olivia had pretended to be disappointed that Nick had never done that for her. Nick had accepted it for the challenge it was, and she could tell by the devilish gleam in his eyes that she was in for a surprise. The next time he was due in she'd rushed home, throwing open the door, expecting to find the place full of big, beautiful balloons—but it was empty except for one pitifully small red balloon tied to the back of a chair. Slowly, her face changing from excitement, disappointment, to intrigued curiosity, Olivia had walked over to read the words painted on it. 'Prick me if you dare.' Smiling now, she'd found a needle and burst the balloon, jumping at the bang. Something fell out and she bent to pick it up. Inside folds of soft tissue paper she found an enamelled brooch. It bore her name in gold letters—surrounded by brightly coloured balloons. Nick had appeared in the doorway to the bedroom, and was watching her. She ran to him, her eyes wet with tears, and threw her arms round his neck. 'Thank you, thank you so much, my darling.'

He had lifted her off her feet and held her close. 'Now you'll always have balloons,' he'd said huskily, and kissed her with a passion that could only have one outcome.

'Perhaps you'd like to see the orangery now?' her guide asked, cutting cruelly into her thoughts. Adding, 'Is anything the matter?'

Olivia blinked rapidly. 'No, of course not. It's just rather cold.'

'Yes. Unfortunately we can't heat the house too much because it warps and splits the furniture, you know. But at least it's stopped raining,' the woman said bracingly. 'You'll be able to see the orangery at its best.'

It was another hour before Olivia was able to get away. The guide had been more than helpful, but then they were everywhere she went once they knew she was writing travel articles for an American magazine. The air smelt fresh and clean after the rain, the strong smells of wet grass and earth filling her senses. Olivia walked slowly down the long driveway to the gate; they had offered to run her back by car but she had refused, wanting some time to herself before she saw Nick again. A river not much bigger than a stream danced and rippled under a Palladian-style bridge that was much too grand for it. Leaning her elbows on the parapet, Olivia wished she were artistic. Maybe she would take it up when she went back to the States; but she would never find scenes like this to paint.

She sighed heavily; everything had seemed so easy before she'd set out for England. All she had to do was find Nick, convince him that she still loved him, and they would go back to the States and settle down, she to her journalistic career and he to flying. In her eager optimism it had all seemed that simple. But that accident had changed Nick, hurt him. It must have been terrible to have lost his father in that way. And yet it hadn't been his fault, so surely he couldn't be blaming himself for it? Olivia frowned, not understanding. How long ago had the accident happened? And what had happened to the plane to cause it to crash? It was possible to find these things out, of course; she could easily make enquiries. But had she the right to do that? Nick had relaxed enough to confide in her a little; oughtn't she to wait until he was ready to tell her more?

Olivia began to walk on again, feeling pressured, thinking that she had so little time. Two weeks had almost gone already, but at least today had been something of a breakthrough. That cheered her, until she remembered that she had soon to face Nick again and decide how she was to act towards him. Until now she had thought it best to treat his injury, and therefore his accident, lightly. But, lord, you couldn't treat anything that involved the death of his father lightly!

He was waiting for her as she had come to expect, leaning against the helicopter, hands in his pockets, apparently no different from any other day. But Olivia had come to read his moods and she could tell by the set of his shoulders that he was bracing himself to meet her. Inspiration came to her and she hurried towards him.

'Oh, Nick, I'm so cold! They had no heating there and I'm sure I've caught a chill. I can't wait to get back to the hotel to take a hot bath.' She shivered and climbed into the chopper as soon as he opened the door. 'You had the best of it today,' she told him when he joined her. 'I wish I'd stayed in the pub by the fire.'

'Didn't you like the house?'

'Oh, yes, it was beautiful.' Her face became pensive. 'All the houses I've seen are beautiful, and full of gorgeous things, but most of them are so—impersonal. I feel as if I'm walking round a museum rather than a home. It's as if they've never been really lived in. And in some places I get to feel as if the visitors are only allowed in on sufferance.'

'I know what you mean,' Nick remarked. 'It's because they want to preserve the houses for posterity, and the only way they can afford to do that is to let in the public, but constant visitors are wearing the places out anyway. It's a catch-22 situation, a battle they can't win.'

'Well, I'm surprised those poor guides don't all suffer from pneumonia,' Olivia said feelingly. 'I feel as if I've got it coming on already.'

'You've led a cosseted life, that's your trouble,' Nick said with a grin. He reached into the map drawer. 'Here, try this.' And he handed her a silver pocket flask.

'Oh, great. I hope it's a hundred per cent proof rye whisky.' It turned out to be brandy, but was just as good. Olivia took a deep draught and offered the flask to Nick. 'Do you want some?'

He shook his head. 'Not after drinking non-alcoholic beer all afternoon.'

'What did you do?' she asked curiously.

'Played darts.'

'You'll have to teach me that.'

Nick raised his eyebrows and switched on the engine, ending the conversation. But Olivia sat back, not bothering to put on her head-set, able to relax now; the tricky moment had passed. They flew back in silence, but it was a comfortable silence, not tense as it easily might have been. She felt tired and closed her eyes, the steady drone of the engines soon sending her to sleep.

The silence woke her. Olivia stirred reluctantly and opened her eyes. They had landed and Nick had switched off the engines and taken off his head-set. He was watching her, his eyes tender, as a father would look at a sleeping child, she thought—and immediately repudiated it. *That* wasn't how she wanted him to look at her. She said, 'Hi,' huskily, and deliberately ran the tip of her tongue across her lips.

His face changed and for a brief moment there was a flash of desire in his eyes, but then Nick turned away and said brusquely, 'We're home.'

She sat up. 'Not for me. I still have to drive into Stratford. How far do you have to go?'

'Only a mile or so.'

'Are you going straight home?'

'No. I still have work to catch up on in the office.'

'Is it my fault?' Olivia asked, getting out.

'No, there's always work to catch up on.' Nick made sure the chopper was securely locked, and carried her bag over to her car for her.

Olivia hesitated, not wanting to leave him, but not knowing how to stay. So instead she just got into the car and said, 'Don't work too hard,' before driving off.

It was ridiculous that she didn't know where he lived, she thought as she drove along. Especially if it was only a mile from the heliport. Being with him in the 'copter had brought her closer to Nick, but it wasn't close enough. She had to find some way to be with him in different surroundings, different circumstances. Coming to the outskirts of the town, she passed a Chinese take-away and a few minuets later turned round and went back to it.

The light was on in Nick's office when she returned half an hour later, a large bag of spicy food and a bottle of wine on the seat of the car beside her. The door to the building was unlocked, and she walked straight in, then leaned against the jamb in the open doorway to his office. 'Hello again,' she said brightly. 'Where would you like it—here, or in Reception?'

Nick had stiffened and was staring at her, a stunned look in his eyes.

'Don't get me wrong,' Olivia added before he could speak. She held out the bag and the bottle. 'I've bought us a Chinese; where do you want to eat it?'

'What the hell did you do that for?' he said roughly.

On an angry, almost defiant note, she answered, 'Because I'm tired of eating alone every night. Because I know we both like Chinese. Because I suddenly felt hungry. It's no big deal.'

Nick continued to look at her for a long moment, then his mouth twisted ruefully. Switching off the computer he was using, he stood up. He didn't apologise but his tone was conciliatory as he asked, 'How can you possibly be hungry after that huge meal you had at lunchtime?'

'I'm always hungry; surely you remember that?'

'You ought to weigh a ton.'

'But I don't.'

'No, you don't.' His eyes ran over her slim figure.

'Well, at least you noticed.' She smiled to take any sarcasm or forwardness out of it. 'Come on, where can we eat?'

'In the rest-room, I suppose.'

Nick led the way out to Reception and through the door on the left. It led to cloakrooms and then a pleasant room with armchairs, a table with half a dozen upright chairs grouped round it, and a television and music-deck in the corner.

'It's where the pilots can relax in between charters,' he explained, drawing peach-coloured curtains across the big picture window. 'Do you want some music?'

'Great.' She looked round. 'I hope you have some plates and forks.'

He found some in a small kitchen opening off the room. 'Here we are, and some glasses for the wine. We'll be able to eat and drink in a civilised manner.'

'Not like that picnic we had that time when we were in Vermont. Do you remember? We forgot the glasses and had to drink champagne out of the bottle.'

'I remember.'

And afterwards they had made love under the trees; did he remember that, too? Perhaps he had, because Nick's tone was brusque and he immediately turned away to find a corkscrew.

'How are your articles going?' he asked, coming to sit opposite her.

A definite change of subject, Olivia thought wryly, but she said, 'OK. I've sent a couple off. One on American connections with Stratford, and the other on the River Avon; its history, the places to see along its banks, hiring boats, that kind of thing.'

'Is that where you've been going on the days you haven't been flying?'

'Yes.' Olivia helped herself to sweet and sour and rice from the foil dishes. 'But I've been driving around the Cotswolds, too.' She paused, a far-away look in her eyes. 'There's something about these hills. I can't explain it. But they fascinate me.'

Nick gave her a quick look. 'A sort of timeless feeling?'

'Yes! Maybe that's it.' She looked at him eagerly. 'Do you feel it, too?'

Before answering, Nick poured wine into their glasses. 'I think I've always felt it; it's bred into me.'

'Why? You don't come from round here, do you?'

'Yes, and my father did, and all his ancestors before him for a few hundred years.'

'But your surname; surely it's French?'

'Yes, but we came over at the time of the Norman Conquest in 1066. So after nine hundred years I think we can safely be classed as of British stock.' His eyes shadowed. 'Or at least I can.'

'Why only you?'

He looked at her contemplatively for a moment then gave an almost imperceptible shrug. 'I'm the last of my line.' Then he laughed in self-mockery. 'What a pretentious thing to say. I just meant that I have no close family now: brothers or sisters, uncles or aunts.' He spoke calmly but there was a note of loneliness in his voice he couldn't hide.

But you could have your own family. The thought leapt to Olivia's mind as it must have been in Nick's. She waited for him to say as much, but when he didn't she avoided the subject and said, 'Can you really trace your roots back to the Norman Conquest?'

It was an idle question but his reply amazed her. 'Oh, yes, there's a family tree in the library that goes right back to...' He paused suddenly, as if he'd inadvertently said something he hadn't meant to, but finished smoothly, 'To the Domesday Book. But it's probably incorrect, of course.' He reached for the dish of prawn balls. 'Have another one of these, they're delicious. Which take-away did you get it all from?'

'A Chinese,' Olivia answered, refusing to be side-tracked. 'Which library is this family tree in? Do you mean the record office in Stratford? I'd like to see it.'

'No, it's in a private library, not open to the public, I'm afraid.'

'How about journalists?'

'No, not open to anyone.'

'Not even to a friend of yours?'

Nick's face hardened. 'Why so interested, Olivia?'

'I'm from the New World; my ancestry only goes back as far as my great-grandfather. I'm overcome with awe at the idea of being able to trace your roots that far back. I'm intrigued. I thought it was only kings and emperors who were able to do that. But if you want to keep it some big secret, then sure. OK. Fine. It's great Chinese and I got it from the restaurant named on the bag. I wish I'd thought to collect a menu so that you could—'

Reaching out, Nick put his hand over hers. 'Olivia, don't. Please. I'm sorry.'

She bit her lip, looking down at his hand, feeling its warmth and strength. Oh, God, I want you, she thought miserably. Putting down her fork, she picked up her glass and took a long swallow, then said brightly, 'No, it's my fault. I never could mind my own business. Just tell me to shut up next time.'

He sat back, taking his hand away, and Olivia felt as if all the warmth had gone out of her heart. 'There's no big secret about it,' he said. 'It's just that the family tree is an old, fragile document that has been shut away for safe keeping.'

'Where's it kept?' Quickly she held up her hand. 'No, don't answer that. Forget I said it. You never talked about your family when we were back in the States.'

Nick shrugged. 'We were always busy, doing other things; I suppose the subject just never came up.'

Olivia tried hard not to think of the other things they'd done, but it wasn't easy. Not the way she felt right now. She felt so *hungry* for love. But only for Nick, only ever for him. And two years was a long time when you were young.

'I take it your divorce went through eventually,' Nick said into the silence.

She gave him a quick look, trying to hide her eagerness. 'Yes, but it was pretty rough. Scott went abroad and I couldn't trace him for months.' Trying to sound casual, she added, 'I thought I wrote and told you that. Oh, no, that's right—you said you moved away and never got my letters.'

After a moment of tense hesitation, Nick said, 'No, that wasn't true. I think I received most of them, if not all.'

Olivia pushed her plate away, giving up the pretence of eating. 'But you wish you hadn't. You wish I'd never written them.'

His voice suddenly harsh, Nick explained, 'I didn't think we'd ever see each other again. I saw little point in continuing to keep in touch. I wrote and told you that. I wanted you to give up any—' his eyes darkened almost as if in pain '—any ideas you might have about our getting together again. It was better to end it completely so that you could—could look for a life with someone else. I wanted you to forget about me. As I had forgotten you,' he added brutally.

Olivia flinched and her cheeks paled. She gave a small, tight smile. 'You were sure determined to get rid of me.'

'Yes.' The one word flicked out like a metal-tipped whip.

Picking up her glass, she held it out. 'Is there any more wine?'

He gave her some, but only half filled the glass. 'That's enough; you have to drive home.'

'Back to the hotel,' Olivia corrected. She ran her fingertip round the rim for a moment or two, then said, 'Those months we were going together may not have meant much to you, Nick. Maybe you have forgotten them—but I haven't. And I'm sorry, but I don't want to. I'd never known what love was until I met you. The memories of the times we were together are very precious to me and—and always will be.' Her voice broke and she looked away. 'Please don't try to spoil them for me.'

She heard him catch his breath, wondered what he would say, but was stunned when he said, his tone sarcastic, 'What you're really saying is that you were ripe for an affair and I came along at the right time. If it hadn't been me it would have been someone else,' he added cruelly. 'Young love, first love, hadn't come up to your expectations and you were starved for sex. I satisfied you and you romanticised it into a big love-affair, when all it really was was a mutually satisfying sexual interlude. Not meant to last or be taken seriously.'

Olivia was staring at him, her face white with shock. Putting her hands under the table, she balled them into tight, nail-hurting fists as she strove to control the hurt, the anger.

'I—I see. So that's all it was for you, was it? A—a sexual interlude?'

'That's what I said.' Nick was watching her steadily, his face a set, grim mask.

'You were tired of me?'

'Yes.'

'And you used the fact that I hadn't got a divorce as an excuse for us to split up?'

'Yes.'

'But why, if you wanted a clean break, didn't you say so at the time? Why leave it—hanging?'

Nick shrugged. 'We'd been good together. I didn't want to hurt you.'

Her eyes came up to meet his. 'Not *then*.'

His brows flickered and he couldn't meet her gaze. 'I thought that writing to end it would be kinder. I didn't expect you to come to England. I didn't think I'd ever see you again. But it's been two years; you can surely take the truth now?'

Olivia's hands were still under the table, but Nick was holding his glass, gripping it, unaware that his knuckles were showing white. His shoulders, too, were tense and his mouth drawn into a grim line. In her line of work you got to study people, watching for their reactions, trying to judge whether they were telling the truth or not. It seemed to Olivia that Nick was displaying an awful lot of tension just to explain his reasons for ditching an old flame two years ago. Getting up, she collected the remains of the food together and carried it into the kitchen.

'Do you have a garbage disposal?'

'Yes, we call them dustmen; they come once a week to collect the rubbish.' Nick had followed her and stood in the doorway.

'"A rose by any other name",' Olivia quoted. 'Do you at least have some coffee?'

'Plenty of that. Why don't you sit down and let me make it?'

'OK.' She went back into the rest-room and sat in one of the armchairs. She was still smarting, but had the feeling that Nick had over-stressed everything; if he really didn't care, surely he wouldn't have been so harsh, so hurtful? This evening certainly wasn't turning out how she had expected it to, she thought with a deep, rueful sigh. But then, a great many things in her life had a habit of not turning out as she'd hoped.

'Are you all right?' The question was asked reluctantly as Nick came in and stood over her, the mugs of coffee in his hands.

'Sure.' She came back fighting and gave him a bright smile.

There was a flicker of admiration in Nick's eyes before he turned and sat down in another chair, a low coffee-table between them. 'What are you doing tomorrow?' he asked, dragging them back to reality.

'Working, I think; that is, writing up notes. But I'll probably walk round the town again, too. I love Stratford. Even if Shakespeare hadn't been born and died there, it would still be a place I could go back to again and again. There's so much going on, in the town and on the river. At night everyone strolls around and I can walk alone without any fear. It's so—' she hunted for a word '—so *English*. Do you know what I mean?'

'I think so. You mean it's possible to see what it was like back through time because the basic structure of an English country market town is still there.'

'Yes. That's exactly it.' She gave a small laugh. 'You always were able to put my thoughts into words better than I could myself.'

Ignoring that, Nick said, 'And what area do you want to cover on our next trip—or have you seen everything you came to see?'

He was giving her a let-out, Olivia realised, in case he had hurt her so much that she didn't want to see him again. But she hadn't given up yet, although she felt bruised and battered. There had been times, like this morning, when she had felt much closer to him, but he seemed to realise this and always kicked her back again. Relaxing her head against the chair, she said, 'I must go to see the prehistoric stone circles at Avebury and Stonehenge in the afternoon, but in the morning I'd like to see the Slad valley—but only if the sun is shining.'

'The weather report is good for the next few days. The Slad valley?' He frowned and then his face cleared. 'Of course; Laurie Lee. You've been reading *Cider with Rosie*.'

'We were made to read it in High School. Only for me it wasn't work; I read the book through a dozen times. I think that's when I first fell in love with the Cotswolds. It was certainly the reason I chose this area to visit and write about now.'

'You and hundreds of thousands of others, I expect. I wonder if the present inhabitants of the valley bless him or curse him?' Nick said musingly.

'Maybe we'll find out.' Olivia looked thoughtful. 'Say, I could work up a piece on that.'

Nick laughed. 'Stealing my ideas now.'

Olivia turned her head and met his eyes. 'It seems that's all you have to give.'

It was Nick who looked away first. He picked up his coffee-cup and drained it. Olivia immediately stood up, knowing what he was going to say, getting in first. 'I must be going.'

'And I must get back to work.' Nick, too, stood up. 'Thanks for the meal.'

Olivia shrugged. She picked up her jacket and went to put it on, but Nick took it from her. 'Let me.'

He helped her on with it, and for a few seconds his hands rested on her shoulders. Tilting her head to look at him, Olivia asked huskily, 'Do you usually eat alone, too?'

His hands tightened momentarily, but then he let her go, saying, 'Don't most single people?'

'Has there been anyone else—for you?' she ventured.

But that was going too far; Nick turned and led the way back into the reception area. 'Sure you're all right to drive?' he asked, holding the door open for her.

'Of course. See you in a couple of days.'

He nodded. 'Goodnight.' And closed the door after her.

Olivia walked slowly to her car. The skies had cleared and the moon and stars were out. The air was full of the scent of rain-clean grass, of wet earth and pine trees. She didn't feel at all tired, and certainly didn't feel like going back to the hotel and tamely going to bed. There were always pubs in the town where she could go and have a drink, she supposed, but being a lone woman in a strange pub wasn't her idea of an enjoyable evening, and it left her open to anyone who thought she might be an easy pick-up. Sexual equality hadn't progressed as far as bars yet, she decided with a sigh. There was the hotel lounge, of course, but that wasn't much better. What she would really like to do was to take a walk, here in this moonlit countryside. But that was out, of course; Nick would be listening for the sound of her car leaving, and might come after her to find out why she hadn't gone. That was almost a tempting idea, but she didn't think she could face an open row with him tonight; their meal together had been emotional enough.

Getting into the car, Olivia reluctantly drove away. She felt a restless kind of anger which she knew from experience was mostly frustration. But tonight it was worse, much worse. To be this close to Nick again was driving her crazy. To love him so much, to want him so badly, and yet to have to pretend otherwise, and to act as if his rejection of her didn't matter. Olivia didn't know how long she could go on, whether in fact it was worth going on pretending; she must have given herself away to him a hundred times already. Certainly Nick was deliberately making it hard for her—throwing out insults, making cruel remarks. Telling her that he had grown tired of her back in New York when all the time she had gone on thinking that there might be some chance for them—that had been particularly cruel. If she believed it; if he was to be believed.

Coming to the main road, Olivia stopped to see if the road was clear. Looking to the left, she remembered that was the way Nick had come on that very first morning when she'd been watching for him. She'd never driven that way, had always turned into the heliport. On impulse she turned left instead of back towards Stratford. Recalling that Nick had said he lived only about a mile away, Olivia set the journey meter and drove slowly along, looking for a likely house. The high wall that edged the grounds surrounding the heliport ran continuously along on her left, on the right there was a hedge dotted with occasional trees that seemed to look out over open fields. After about three-quarters of a mile the wall on the left was broken by wide wrought-iron gates set under an elaborate stone arch. There was a worn sign, which she could just make out, that said, 'Harnbury Hall'. Beyond it, on the other side of the road, there was another driveway and a much smarter sign saying, 'Harnbury Farm, Bed & Breakfast'. Neither of these seemed particularly likely. The mile was up but Olivia drove on for a further mile, but all she passed were more open fields and trees.

Puzzled, she came to a stop; surely Nick couldn't be lodging at the farm? But it was certainly convenient for the heliport, and presumably they would provide him with an evening meal as well as breakfast, if he wanted it. Pushing her other feelings out of her mind, Olivia let curiosity take over. Turning the car, she drove back past the heliport, then turned again and parked on the grass verge. Switching off her lights she settled down to wait; she hadn't passed any cars on her search so presumably Nick must still be working—unless of course he'd decided to go the other way tonight, into Stratford. In which case she was in for a long, long wait. That would be silly; deciding to give him an hour, Olivia switched on the radio, found some music, and sat back in her seat.

Her thoughts immediately flew back to earlier that evening, and she couldn't drag them away. Nick was behaving so strangely; she just couldn't fathom him. At one moment he seemed to hate her, but then he would give himself away and she'd be sure that he wasn't as immune to her as he made out. Was she beating her head against a stone wall, Olivia wondered, the stone wall that Nick seemed to have built so thickly round himself? For the thousandth time she asked herself why, why had he changed so much? With anyone else she would have guessed at an unhappy love-affair to make him so bitter, to act as if he hated all women. But Nick hadn't answered her when she'd asked him if there had been anyone else in his life since her. Was that a good sign or a bad? On the whole, good, she decided. If there had been someone else, surely he would have said so, in the hope that it would make her finally decide to give up on him and go.

But thinking about that did nothing but give her a headache. It didn't seem likely, but possibly it had something to do with his plane crash. Maybe it wouldn't hurt to do a little investigating in that direction. Olivia remembered the photos and mementos on Nick's wall; perhaps if she looked at them more closely they would give her a clue.

She had begun to list in her mind what other lines she could follow when she saw Nick's car appear at the entrance. He got out of the car, closed the gates behind him and locked them before getting in the car again. Olivia waited breathlessly, watching to see which way he would go. He turned left. When he reached the first bend, she put on her lights and followed him. Nick drove quite quickly, sure of his way, his headlights cutting a swath of light between the wall and the hedge, and she had to go faster to keep him in sight. But then she had to brake when he slowed right down as the two driveways approached. Olivia expected him to swing right into the farm, and her mouth dropped open in surprise when he turned the other way and stopped in front of the big iron gates. Hastily she slowed down to a crawl and watched as he waited for a moment, the gates swung open, and Nick drove through.

By the time Olivia reached the entrance the gates were starting to close. She parked the car and walked carefully back, keeping near the wall. The gates shut smoothly, with only a small clicking sound. They must be operated electronically from a gadget in Nick's car, she realised. Going up to them, Olivia looked through the swirling iron-work and saw the tail-lights of Nick's car winking as they passed the trunks of large trees before they disappeared altogether. She put her hands on the gates and tried to push them open, searched for a latch, but they were locked fast. It would be possible to climb them, she supposed, peering upwards, but they looked awfully high.

She stepped back and looked at the sign, faded by sunlight and age. 'Harnbury Hall'. This, then, was the place where Nick must live, but it was still as much of a mystery as ever. With a small sigh of defeat, Olivia got back into the car and drove away.

CHAPTER SIX

THE Slad valley lay on the western edge of the Cotswolds, in Gloucestershire. There were thick woods here, more than in any other part of the area that Olivia had seen, but it was the meadows that drew her, in every shade of green, and the farmhouses set in hollows and the long lines of stone walls that edged the narrow country lanes. It almost looked like a painting of a perfect landscape until she saw a tractor working in a field, and a herd of sheep being driven along a lane and swirling like a snowdrift round a car that had stopped for them to pass.

Olivia sighed with pleasure. 'It's just as I imagined it. What a wonderful place for a child to grow up in, even now. It must be even more beautiful in the summer.'

'You shouldn't be seeing it from up here,' Nick told her. 'You should go there, and then leave the car and walk. You New Yorkers never walk anywhere if you can ride.'

'I used to jog in Central park every morning,' Olivia returned indignantly, used by now to talking to him via the head-set.

'I never saw you jog.'

She paused but then said, 'I guess that was because I never got up very early when you were around.'

He gave her a fleeting glance, and she could visibly see the tension rise in him. 'No, I suppose not. Do you want to land?'

'Will you walk with me?'

He shook his head. 'I've brought some work with me I can do while I wait.'

'I'll leave it, then. Maybe I'll drive here tomorrow.' They flew on a little further and Olivia pointed to a spread of buildings on the horizon. 'What town is that?'

'It's Stroud.'

'Is it worth seeing?'

'Painswick is better. It has a beautiful church and it's set on a hillside so you have steep lanes and narrow alleys. And it hasn't changed so much; there aren't any shops with plate-glass windows. The buildings are all of stone, a sort of grey colour; the same stone they used to build Gloucester Cathedral.'

'Can we fly over it?'

'Sure.'

Olivia got her camera set but she knew she wouldn't be able to get good pictures; she was constantly frustrated that Nick couldn't fly low over towns and other built-up areas. The setting of the town was beautiful, the surrounding meadows coming right up to the houses. Olivia took several shots and determined to visit the town again the next day. 'It's beautiful. A perfect place,' she said sincerely.

'Maybe I shouldn't have shown it to you,' Nick remarked.

'Why on earth not?'

'Because there's just one thing wrong with Painswick, and I've an idea your travel articles are probably going to add to it. There are too many tourists visiting the town already. In the summer it's choked with cars, almost as busy as Broadway. The age-old problem.'

'The twentieth-century problem,' Olivia corrected. 'I shouldn't have thought there were many tourists around before everyone had cars.'

'Another article for you,' Nick said lightly. 'On nine-teenth-century tourists.'

'You seem to enjoy finding work for me,' she said in teasing complaint. She turned to glance at him specula-tively before saying, 'At this rate I'll never go home.'

Nick had nothing to say about that. He became intent on his flying as they carried on along the Slad valley in the other direction, over a dozen pretty villages that Olivia promised herself to visit the next day, but sadly knew that she'd never have time to do them all. Some twenty minutes later, when they left the valley, Nick said, 'Avebury and Stonehenge?'

'Please.'

He nodded, and headed south.

The two ancient stone circles were another treat that Olivia had saved for a sunny day. They went to Avebury, the nearer of the two, first, and Olivia was amazed to find the stone circle so large that a village had been built in the middle. They landed and walked first to an old barn converted into a quaint restaurant.

Nick looked inside and said, 'Are you sure you want to eat here? They do food at the pub.'

'Yes, I'm sure. This will make a change.'

They had soup and a salad, then Olivia set off to walk round the circle alone. The stones weren't terribly large and a great many of them had been lost or buried since they were set up in the early Bronze Age, but there were painted maps on posts at intervals telling you all about them. She tried to lose herself in them, to feel the spirit of the place, but the village was too close, the stones too worn; she couldn't conjure up any mental pictures of the men who had erected them. Hands in pockets, Olivia strolled back to the village and was seduced into going round the local manor house to look at the furniture and porcelain of the eighteenth and nineteenth centuries instead. Returning to the chopper, she was attracted by the windows of a gift shop, and came out some twenty minutes later having bought a water-divining kit.

Nick was sitting on the ground under a tree, a little distance from the chopper, his open briefcase beside him. But he was reading a book.

'I thought you said you had work to do?' Olivia chided, dropping down beside him.

'You've been so long that I've finished it.'

'What are you reading?' She leant across him to look at the title. *'Cider with Rosie!* Haven't you ever read it before?'

'Of course. I just thought that today would be a good time to read it again. What's that you've got?'

'It's a water-diviner. It seems that you just have to hold it and if there's water under the ground it will shake like mad.'

'And just what use do you think you're going to make of that in New York? Somehow I don't think it's capable of working through solid concrete.'

Olivia wrinkled her nose at him. 'Don't be such a spoilsport. Come on, let's have a go.' She took the kit, a piece of wood which opened out into two short branches, from the packet and began to walk around, holding it pointed at the ground.

'You've got to have a natural talent for it. You've either got it or you haven't,' Nick informed her.

'So I'm about to find out.'

Nick watched her for a few more minutes, then said, 'You're doing it all wrong. Hold it level and wait for it to dip.'

'Nothing's happening. Perhaps there isn't any water near here.'

'You're not holding it right.'

'OK, know-all, come and show me how,' Olivia returned exasperatedly.

Getting to his feet, Nick came over and took it from her. 'Hold it like this.' He put his hands under the two branches of the twig instead of on top. 'Now you try.'

Olivia did as he'd shown her, but, still not satisfied, Nick came behind her and reached round to put his hands over hers. 'Like this.'

They walked together for several yards when the twig suddenly began to shake violently and dip towards the ground.

'It works! Wow, it works. We've found water!' She was thrilled with excitement and for a moment didn't realise that Nick was shaking with suppressed mirth. Then she let go of the twig and turned suddenly within the circle of his arms to see the laughter in his face. 'You louse! You made it shake.' She thumped him on the chest. 'I really thought I'd got the talent, that I'd made it go.'

Nick was openly laughing. 'You may have many talents, my sweet, but water-divining definitely isn't one of them.'

Her hands resting on his chest, Olivia looked up at him. Her voice suddenly husky, she said, 'What talents had you in mind?'

The laughter faded from Nick's face as he gazed down at her. Dropping the diviner, he put his hands up to cover hers, his eyes darkening with desire. For a moment, for a glorious, wonderful moment, she thought that he was going to kiss her as his hands tightened. But then he roughly thrust her away. Unbalanced, Olivia stepped back and felt something crack beneath her foot. She turned, glad of the excuse, letting her hair fall and hide her face. She'd trodden on the diviner.

'Oh, it's broken.' She bent to pick it up.

'It's my fault, I'm sorry. I'll buy you another,' Nick said harshly, his voice charged with tension.

'Don't be silly. It was only a toy.' She threw the broken twig into a hedge. 'What's the time? Hadn't we better get going?'

They walked back to the chopper in silence. Nick shooed away some village children who'd come to take a closer look and they flew off again.

The light was bright and they were both wearing sunglasses. Which of us is hiding? Olivia thought miserably. Probably both of us. But at least he had teased her and they'd laughed together. And she ought to have known he'd push her away—one step forward, one push back. She gazed out of the windscreen, apparently absorbed in the scenery, but too full of her own thoughts to notice anything until they reached Stonehenge.

It was set almost in the centre of what must once have been a huge open plain, bisected now by roads. The great standing stones, much more impressive than those at Avebury, were massive in size and better preserved. Olivia had arranged her visit in advance, and a young man in uniform came to meet them. He brightened perceptibly when he took in Olivia's attractive face and figure.

'Welcome to Stonehenge. You're in luck; most of the tourists have left for the day, so we'll have it almost to ourselves.'

He took her on a very leisurely tour, enjoying having a pretty girl to air his knowledge to. Olivia didn't mind if it meant that she got more information, but she moved away after he'd put his hand on her arm a few times to draw her towards particular stones. 'Where are you staying?' he asked her, obviously leading up to making a pass.

'In Stratford-upon-Avon—with my boyfriend. He's the one flying the chopper.'

That message got through and her guide soon found that he had to get back to his office. Left on her own, Olivia wandered, able now to feel the spirit of the place, to hear the voice of history. She sat on a slight mound, looking back at the stones as they cast long shadows in the late afternoon sunlight. The story the guide had told her, of thousands of men struggling to bring the huge monoliths here by land and sea, to erect them and top them with massive lintels to form this giant circle in this vast open plain, filled her mind with awe. If she closed her eyes she could almost see them, driven by the same religious fervour to build huge temples to their gods that had also driven the Egyptians, the Greeks, the Romans, and even the Incas in far away South America. Like ants they had laboured and like ants they had been forgotten, but their temple still stood for modern man to gaze and wonder at.

It made Olivia feel very small, her problems insignificant. What the hell did she matter in the general scheme of things? So what if the man she loved had ditched her? There was no one in the world to care. Olivia wasn't the crying type; even when Nick had left her she hadn't cried, because she'd thought it was all a mistake and would soon be sorted out, and she'd had hope then, of course. But now, stupidly, tears began to flow down her cheeks. She couldn't stop them so she let them fall, and sat quietly, her hands clasped round her knees.

'Olivia?' Nick had walked silently over and gave an exclamation of dismay when he saw that she was crying. Dropping down to his knees, he put an arm round her. 'Oh, don't! I'm sorry, I'm so sorry, but please don't cry.'

'I can't—I can't help it.' She opened her eyes to find Nick gazing at her in raw, tortured pain.

'For pity's sake, Olivia, please stop. I can't bear to see you cry.'

'*You* can't bear it!' Suddenly, gloriously, she was full of surging anger. 'Good grief, you don't think I'm crying because of you, do you?' She jumped to her feet, shoving Nick aside so roughly that he almost overbalanced. 'I've *never* cried over you!'

She began to stride away from him, but he quickly came after her and caught her arm. His eyes searching her face suspiciously, he asked, 'Then just why are you crying?'

'Because of *that.*' She flung out her free arm to point at Stonehenge. 'Because it's so beautiful in the evening light. Because it's so old.'

'And that makes you cry as if your heart is breaking?' Nick said disbelievingly.

'Yes! Looking at it, it makes you realise just how unimportant you are. And how—how pointless it all is,' she finished on a bitter note.

'What's pointless?'

She turned to glare at him, the sun catching her hair, touching it with flame. 'Life. Love. All the petty little problems. Everything.'

Afraid of crying again, Olivia tried to pull away from him, but Nick held her fast. 'It isn't like you to let things get to you like this.'

'How the hell would you know what I'm like?' she retorted violently.

'Of course I know.'

'All right, I'll re-phrase it—what the hell do you *care* what I'm like?' Her voice had risen and she was yelling at him, close to hysteria.

Nick caught hold of her shoulders and stared tensely into her face. 'Of course I damn well care about you.'

A shudder ran through her and Olivia gave a great sob. 'Well, you've a crazy way of showing it.'

He pulled her to him and held her close, his arms comforting by their strength, held her until her trembling eased. Only then did Olivia look up at him, her lashes still wet, her eyes vulnerable, almost afraid. 'Oh, Nick, I've never felt so alone in all my life as I did sitting there.' She groped for words to express her feelings. 'I felt as if I'd lost all hope, lost all the purpose in life.'

'You let the sadness of the place get to you.'

Looking over her shoulder at the stones, Olivia said, 'Is it sad?'

'A ruin is always sad.'

'Yes, I suppose so. But these stones are triumphant too; don't you feel that?'

'A triumph of man's endeavour over overwhelming difficulties, you mean?'

'Yes.' She gave a small laugh. 'That's rather the way I feel, too, at the moment.' He went to let her go at that, but she put her arms round his neck. 'Please kiss me, Nick.'

'Olivia.' There was a heavy note of reproach in his voice.

'You just said that you care for me.'

'Care *about* you,' he corrected.

'It's the same thing.'

'No, it—'

But Olivia impatiently reached up to put a hand on either side of his head and kiss him.

For a few seconds he resisted her. He gave a groan of protest and reached up to grab her arms and pull them down, but she clung to him, her mouth avidly seeking his. Nick groaned again, but now it was on an entirely different note as he suddenly put his arms around her and held her close against him. And then it was he who took over, who bent her against his length so that she could feel his body harden with need, who took her mouth in fierce, starved passion. Olivia gave a cry of infinite gratitude and surrendered completely to his male dominance, letting herself drown in the wonder of being back in his arms, of the glory of his lips as she opened her mouth under the onslaught of his. The yearning ache of need, that was never far away, rose to engulf her, burning like a flame, searing through her veins.

She moaned under his mouth, pressed her hips in agonising longing against his, driving him frantic. 'Oh, Nick, Nick. It's been so long.'

He put a hand low on her waist and threw back his head, giving a hoarse cry of rising excitement. But then Nick was kissing her again with feverish savagery, raining kisses on her eyes, her throat, his breath coming in short, gasping moans, his hand clumsy at her breast.

'My darling, my love.' Olivia returned his kisses ardently, almost fiercely, oblivious to everything except his closeness. 'Oh, Nick, honey, I love you so much, so much.'

Her eyes were closed, and Olivia was completely unprepared when Nick suddenly gripped her shoulders and pushed her away from him. She gazed at him uncomprehendingly, sagging in his hold, her eyes alight with radiant love and desire.

'Oh, hell! Oh, hell, no.' Nick ground out the words, his face dark and tormented. Abruptly letting her go, he turned and strode away.

Off balance, Olivia staggered and almost fell, but then she was running after him, reaching out to catch his arm. 'Nick, wait! What is it? What's the matter?'

'Go home, Olivia. For God's sake go home.'

'No! What are you talking about? Nick, stop.'

But he went charging on, making her run to keep up with him. His face was working with emotion, his eyes agonised, but his jaw was thrust forward in fierce determination.

Running in front of him, Olivia held her arms out and made him stop. She stood panting, trying to get back her breath, searching his face. 'Why do you want me to go home? What was so wrong in wanting to kiss you? What did I do?'

'It wasn't your fault, it was mine. I should never have—' Nick broke off, shaking his head, unable to go on. Tentatively, Olivia put a hand on his arm, gazing at him pleadingly, but then he seemed to make a massive inner effort and he straightened up, his face hard, his raw emotions back under control. 'Go home, Olivia. There's nothing here for you.'

'It didn't seem like that a minute ago.' She spoke disbelievingly, the urgency of his desire having brought back her confidence.

'That was—a mistake.'

She gazed at him, feeling suddenly afraid again. Gropingly she said, 'You know I love you. You know that's why I came here. There—there hasn't been anyone else, Nick. Not since you left.'

Briefly his eyes came up to meet hers, bleak, angry, sad. 'I have nothing to give you,' he said savagely.

Taken aback by his violence, Olivia could only say, 'But—all I want is you.'

Reaching out, he took hold of her shoulders again and gave her an angry shake. 'Why won't you listen to me? You must go back to the States. I don't want you any more.'

'Yes, you damn well do,' she returned heatedly. 'You just proved that.'

A hunted look came into Nick's eyes, but he insisted fiercely, 'You're wrong! I want you out of my life.'

He began to walk on again, but she ran and caught him up. 'But why? What's changed? Why are you being like this?'

He kept on walking. 'I have my own life to live—and it doesn't include you. You should never have come here.'

'But what's happened to you? If something's wrong, why don't you come straight out and tell me?'

'Nothing's wrong,' he said dismissively.

'Yes, there darn well is.' She swung him round to face her. 'You can't hide the way you feel about me, Nick, any more than I can hide the way I feel about you. You *know* I love you. You've probably known from the minute I walked into your office. And you've known that this would happen, too. What we had together was too good, too strong for us to go on behaving as if nothing had happened, as if we didn't still love each other.'

His eyes grew cold. 'You can speak about your own feelings, if you must, but don't try to describe mine.'

'I don't have to describe them; you showed how much you needed me back there when you kissed me.'

He seemed to flinch for a second but then his face tightened as Nick said sardonically, 'Not *you* particularly—any woman would have done.'

She gasped and let him go, stunned by his cruelty. He strode on, heading towards the chopper. In angry frustration, Olivia called after him, 'You don't ring true, Nick. You can't care about me one moment and then be this cruel the next.'

He reached the helicopter, unlocked the door and climbed in, then turned to face her. 'I can be anything I damn well want to be. And what I want right now is to be free of you!'

Olivia stood in the grass, staring across at him, almost expecting him to fly off and leave her. The sun was starting to set, turning the sky to flame and gold. The dying rays lay across her, outlining the bones of her face and the curves of her body, casting a long, sharp shadow that swayed a little as she waited. Nick put on his headset, then turned to look down at her. 'Are you coming?'

Olivia would have liked to tell him to go to hell, but found she had no pride left. Walking round the chopper, she got in the other side and closed the door. Nick reached across to check it, as he always did, and she flinched away, not wanting him to touch her, however accidentally. Nick's hand stilled, briefly, and then he sat back, his profile set in lines of adamant withdrawal.

They passed within range of an airfield on the way home, and Nick spoke briefly on the radio. 'This is helicopter Golf, Victor Alpha Uniform X-ray. Evesham Helicopter Services. Two people on board. Requesting flight information service.' He thanked the radio operator and that was all he said the whole journey.

Olivia leaned back in her seat, feeling strangely numb. Again things hadn't worked out the way she had hoped. At least, not entirely. That kiss had worked out better than she'd dared to dream until Nick had walked away from it. She had been so exultant then, sure that he hadn't stopped loving her. But he had ruined everything of course, as he always seemed to do nowadays. Stealing a look at him under her lashes, Olivia wondered if he could possibly have really meant it when he'd said that *any* woman would do. He'd sure as hell acted extremely frustrated, almost as if he, too, had had no one else since they'd parted. But that was too much to hope for, Olivia decided. Nick had always been a very virile man and there was no reason why he shouldn't have had other women. After all, she thought bitterly, he was free; there had been no promises of undying faithfulness between them. That she had chosen to live as if there had been was entirely her own responsibility.

Would he be willing to be her pilot any more? she wondered. And, even more important, would she want him to after today? But she knew she would. Her pride seemed to have taken so many knocks in the last weeks that at the moment it had disappeared altogether. They approached the heliport in the last light of evening, and she noticed the gabled roofs of the big house she had seen before. Forgetting her troubles for a moment, Olivia pointed down. 'Can we fly over that house? It looks beautiful with the sun reflecting off all those latticed windows.'

'Sorry, no,' he replied curtly.

She gave him a reproachful look. 'It wouldn't hurt you to fly over it.'

'I'm not allowed to. The place is falling apart and the vibration from the rotor blades would probably be the last straw.' He glanced at her. 'It's part of my agreement with the owner.'

She nodded, accepting his explanation, and stayed silent until they had landed and Bill Fairford came over to help her out.

'You're late back tonight,' he commented.

She managed a smile for him as he helped her with her bag of cameras. 'Yes. It's been—a long day.' She turned to look at Nick, met his eyes squarely. 'Good-night, Nick. I'll see you on Monday. You haven't forgotten I want to go to Lindisfarne? You said we'd have to make an early start?'

Nick hesitated, seemed about to speak, but changed his mind when he realised that Bill was still there. 'Haven't you seen enough yet?' he compromised.

'No.' Her chin came up. 'We signed a contract; *I* don't intend to go back on it.'

He frowned but could do little more than nod. 'All right. We'll need to start about six in the morning.'

'I'll be here.' And she walked quickly over to her car and drove away.

That weekend Olivia spent driving round the west Cotswolds, trying to visit all the places she'd seen from the air. The early spring was proving to be almost as hot as summer. Everywhere flowers were coming into early bloom and birds were singing their hearts out as they built their nests in trees and hedgerows that were bursting into leaf. It was a time of optimistic renewal; there were lambs and calves in the fields, young foals on wobbly legs standing alongside their mothers in the fenced paddocks. Olivia looked at them with jealous eyes. It's the mating season and I'm the only one without a mate, she thought with an inner laugh of chagrin at her own frustration.

Feeling in a gloomy mood, she turned off the main road and followed meandering lanes to tiny villages of only thirty or so houses, each with its lichen-roofed busstop and tiny church, the graveyards full of table-top tombs casting peaceful shadows in the sun. A good place to lie, she thought, where others had been laid for centuries of time. Then, angry at herself for getting morbid, Olivia jumped in the car and drove to Painswick, where she joined the window-shoppers strolling the High Street, poked around antique shops, and bought apples for a belated lunch from a market stall. In the evening she went to the theatre in Stratford again, the Royal Shakespeare this time, made herself known to the manager, and told him she would like to do a feature on the two theatres. He was as helpful as everyone else she'd met, and invited her to come to a rehearsal one morning when she was free.

Sunday she went exploring again, but the weather wasn't so warm and there were less people around. Usually just walking or driving through the little villages and pretty towns made her feel at peace, but today she felt overpoweringly lonely. Stopping outside a church that the guide book said had a fourteenth-century wall-painting, Olivia waited outside for a service to end before she could go in and explore. Her thoughts went to Nick, as they always did, and she wondered what he was doing today. Was he flying? He'd said that he often worked harder during the weekends than he did in the week. Olivia looked up at the sky, almost as if she expected to see a helicopter beating its way through the scudding clouds. You fool, Nick, she thought with sudden vehemence. What the hell's the matter with you?

Suddenly deciding that she couldn't just sit there for half an hour with nothing to do but think, Olivia turned the car and headed purposefully back to Harnbury-on-the-Wold and the heliport. But as she neared the village she slowed right down; what would be the good of confronting Nick again? They'd probably only have another fight that might finish everything between them, and so long as there was even one fragile thread to hold on to she would cling to it like grim death.

The entrance to Harnbury Hall, the massive stone gateway that Nick had driven through the other night, came into sight. Impulsively, Olivia parked the car and walked over to it. Again the gates were locked. There was a bell-push and one of those grilles that you spoke into set into the pillar on the left, and she was strongly tempted to press it. But what if Nick answered? What was she supposed to do—say, 'Sorry, wrong number,' or something? Olivia began to walk along the wall in the opposite direction to the heliport, but there was no other gate and no place where she could climb over. Although there was the other gate that led to the heliport, of course. Maybe that had once been the tradesmen's entrance to the Hall; nearly all the mansions that Olivia had seen in England had had a secondary entrance of some kind.

Eagerly she went back to the car, drove further down the road and parked again. The gates were open. Good. That must mean that Nick was working. Running through them, Olivia took to the trees, ready to hide if Nick or anyone came along, but there was no one about and she safely passed the turn-off for the heliport and kept going down the lane. She was sure that this must have been a part of the avenue leading from the gate because the trees, mostly limes, she thought, continued on either side. They were only broken where the tarmac road went off to the heliport.

But it didn't look as if the road was used very much. It soon became overgrown and broken, with grass pushing through the surface and rhododendron bushes that had been let go wild, clawing their way towards the centre. Olivia had only gone a couple of hundred yards when she found the reason for the road's lack of use; one of the

huge trees had fallen, completely blocking the way, and
bringing down a couple of smaller trees with it. She went
round the huge ball of earth, higher than her head, pulled
up by the roots of the fallen tree, and continued down the
avenue. Eight more trees blocked the way, and some had
fallen from the other side of the avenue, too, as if some
great force had blown them down.

The avenue was almost a mile long and was, as Olivia
had thought, a tradesmen's entrance. At its end she found
herself at the entrance to what must once have been a
large and busy stable yard. Now the doors under a stone
bell-tower were closed, the stalls empty, so she carried on,
went round the corner of the wall—and came to a complete halt. Ahead of her was the house that she'd seen
from the air, standing tall and golden and graceful, with
mullioned windows reflecting the light and high Tudor
chimneys reaching up into the sky. Olivia caught her
breath, entranced by the sight, and walked nearer, fascinated, feasting her eyes on the beauty of the building.

She tried to think if she had read anything about the
house in her guide book, but then remembered that Nick
had said it belonged to a private owner. Lucky man, to
own this, she thought, and a rich one, too. But as she
walked out from the trees, Olivia saw that the garden
around the house was unkempt, the topiary-work re-
verting to bushes, the archways of climbing roses left long
unpruned, and the trees beyond becoming a jungle. In
the windows of the house, too, there were broken panes
that had been boarded up from the inside, and some of
the stonework was cracked and in one place had broken
away. It looked empty, deserted and uncared for. Olivia
felt a great surge of pity for the house. Whoever owned
it ought to be shot, she thought angrily. Fancy letting it
get into this state.

Walking up to the house, she tried to peer through the windows, putting up her hand to shield her eyes, but most of them either had curtains pulled across or had inside shutters that left no gaps for her to see through. Only at one window, on the side of the house, could she see in. The room was large but by no means huge. It had an ornate plaster ceiling from what she could see, and there was a carved stone fireplace against the left hand wall with the built-up ash of many fires in the grate. An armchair was pulled up to the fire and beside it there was a table stacked with books and magazines, as if whoever sat there spent long hours reading. But there was only one chair. Puzzled, Olivia drew back. She was about to continue walking round the house, peering through the ground-floor windows, when she heard the sound of a car approaching. Hurriedly, afraid of being caught trespassing, she ran back to the trees and hid behind the huge trunk of an old oak. A familiar car came into sight and Olivia gasped with astonishment as Nick got out, walked up to the house—and without hesitation let himself in by the main door.

CHAPTER SEVEN

LOOKING out of the window when she got out of bed at five the next morning, Olivia found the weather grey and overcast. But it wasn't raining and the sky looked lighter on the horizon. Ever optimistic, Olivia took a hot and then cold shower to wake herself up. Last night hadn't been a restful one; she had been too intrigued by the puzzle of Nick's being at that beautiful old house to sleep very well. She dressed, made herself a coffee and ate some of the biscuits provided by the hotel; the kitchen, she knew, wouldn't be open for breakfast this early in the day. She was half expecting a phone call from Nick to say that the flight was off because of the weather, but none came by five-thirty so she put on a warm anorak over her sweater and jeans and drove out to Harnbury.

Although the roads were empty there was a ghostly kind of mist spreading from the fields once she had left the town behind, making her drive slowly and carefully. It was patchy, though, so she arrived at the heliport on time. The gates were open and she found Nick in his office, the light on, dealing with some paperwork.

'Don't you ever stop working?' she asked him.

'Just writing out the week's schedule. I do it every Monday morning.'

He didn't look up from the chart that he was filling in with pilots' names and jobs, so Olivia went to sit in the chair on the other side of his desk. She watched him, wondering if he was going to behave as if their last confrontation hadn't occurred. She had mixed feelings about it herself, at one moment wishing it had never happened, but at the next supremely thankful for that kiss.

Trying to push it out of her mind, she leaned to take a closer look at the photographs on the wall. Mostly they were just of the old biplane, but there was one of Nick standing beside a middle-aged man who bore a strong resemblance to him and who she guessed must be his father, and another of the same man standing alone with the plane.

Nick reached to pick up something from his desk and, afraid that he might catch her, Olivia quickly turned away and said, 'Will we be able to fly this morning, with the mist?'

'It's only a ground mist and it's due to clear in about thirty minutes.'

'I could have had another half-hour in bed,' she remarked wistfully.

Nick glanced at her. 'If I'd phoned to tell you about the delay you would have been awake anyway, so what was the point?'

Feelingly, Olivia said, 'I hate men when they're logical.'

His lips quirked a little but no way could you call it a smile. But it was better than nothing. Olivia sat quietly in her chair, waiting, and tried to use mental telepathy to let him know that she loved and needed him. It didn't work of course; Nick just went on stolidly filling in his chart, and completely ignored her until he'd finished. It was warm in the office and he'd taken off his jacket. Under it he was wearing a crisp blue shirt and a tie with his company's logo on it, the twined initials EHS for Evesham Helicopter Services and a little chopper underneath in gold. The colour suited him, but then Olivia couldn't remember him wearing a colour he didn't look good in.

Nick looked at his watch and then walked to the window to look up at the sky. 'It's clearing; we may as well get going.' He picked up a navy sweater, again with the logo embroidered on it, and put it on the way men did, pushing his arms into the sleeves first. I wonder why women never do that? Olivia mused. Then he put on the leather jacket that he normally wore. Glancing at her feet, clad in comfortable trainers, he said, 'Have you brought some boots?'

'Boots? No. Should I have done?'

'You'll probably get your feet wet.' He pursed his lips. 'I've an idea Jane keeps a pair here. Hang on, I'll have a look.'

He came back a few minutes later with a pair of green Wellingtons. 'See if these fit.'

Olivia pulled off a trainer and tried one on. 'They're a bit big.'

'I'll lend you an extra pair of socks; I keep some here.' He rummaged in the bottom drawer of his desk and pulled a pair out for her.

'Thanks.' Olivia took them, thinking that for someone who wanted her out of his life he was very solicitous about her comfort. 'Will Jane mind me borrowing the boots?'

'No, I'm sure she won't, but I'll leave her a note just in case she looks for them.'

He carried her boots and some for himself over to his helicopter. They always used the same one, G-VAUX, his call sign and of course the letters of his surname, specially built for Nick after his accident. As he'd said, the

mist had evaporated a lot, but it was still cloudy as they
lifted off and headed north-east.

They had a long way to go. Lindisfarne was almost on
the border with Scotland, and by car would have meant
an overnight trip, but the chopper flew happily on in a
straight line, cocking a snook at clogged motorways and
red lights. Around nine they stopped to re-fuel and had
coffee from a flask that Nick had brought with him, taking it in turn to use the cup lid. The sky had cleared a lot
by now, but it was windy, the clouds racing across the
blue sky. It felt cooler, too, and Olivia was glad of the hot
drink as they stood waiting for the chopper's tanks to be
refilled.

When they reached the coast Nick flew along it, over
the sea. It was the first time Olivia had flown over the
ocean in a chopper, and she caught her breath, not sure
if she liked it. Some islands with a lighthouse appeared
out to sea and Nick pointed. 'Those are the Farne islands.'

'Is that where we're going?'

'No, Lindisfarne is on Holy Island.'

'Are those islands deserted? Can we fly over them so I
can take some pictures?'

'I'm not sure if anyone lives there now, but we can't go
there; they're bird and seal sanctuaries.'

They flew on a little further, and Olivia's mouth
opened in wonder as she saw an island rising up out of
the sea, surmounted by an ancient castle at the very peak
of the mound. 'That's Holy Island?'

'That's it. And the castle is Lindisfarne.'

'It looks so wild, so romantic,' Olivia breathed in fascinated awe. 'Think what it must be like in a storm.' Then
she gave an exclamation of amazement. 'Hey, look!
There are cars driving through the sea.'

Nick grinned. 'It's a causeway. And we have to follow it out to the island so I can find the place where we're to land.'

He flew inland, picked up the sea-bound causeway and turned to follow it, racing the cars. They landed in a field near the carpark, but it was a good half-mile from the castle itself. To reach it you had to walk along a sandy track with deep puddles of water left by rain and sea-spray, so Olivia was grateful for the boots. To her surprise, Nick came with her, and she took advantage of his tall figure beside her to help shelter her from the wind. It was much stronger here by the sea, and was blowing from their right, so Nick walked on that side and carried her camera-bag so that she could hold her collar up with both hands. There was no one else around; they—and the high, raucous gulls that dipped and wheeled with the wind—had the place to themselves.

The castle doorway was reached by a steep, wet staircase of stone and cobbled steps. There was a handrail, but Olivia could imagine it being lethal to anyone old or unsteady on their legs trying to come down it. But inside it was a different world, warm and inviting. The curator, who had opened the castle especially for her, made them welcome with a glass of sherry that went down like nectar after the cold outside, then took her on a tour round. And Nick came too. Something that so pleased her that for a few minutes Olivia couldn't concentrate as their guide explained that the sixteenth-century castle, built to guard the island from attack, had been converted in 1903 into a holiday home.

'A holiday home? This?' Olivia stared in surprise. She looked round the hall with its deep windows and huge fireplace. 'Some weekend cottage!'

Both men laughed at her stunned expression. 'Well, it was converted for the owner by Sir Edwin Lutyens and the garden designed by Gertrude Jekyll,' their guide told her.

Olivia knew enough by now to know that these were *the* names in early twentieth-century architecture and gardening. She looked around her with greater interest and asked the right kind of questions, judging from the pleased look on the curator's face. He introduced them to his wife, and Olivia took their photo, perhaps to illustrate her article. Afterwards they went out to see the garden, which was sheltered from the wind, but it had veered and caught them squarely in the face when they said goodbye to their host and began the walk back. After a couple of hundred yards Olivia looked back and stopped.

'I'd like to take a picture from here.' She got out her camera, took a couple of shots, then turned to Nick. 'Would you stand in the picture so that I can get some perspective?'

He raised an eyebrow but did as she asked, but he became impatient when she moved him around. 'Make up your mind, woman; I need a drink from that pub we passed in the village.'

'You know something? I'm beginning to think you're a lush.'

Nick gave her a surprised look and laughed, so Olivia got the shot she wanted.

'Would you like one of both of you together?'

She turned in surprise, not having heard the middle-aged, friendly-looking woman who had come up behind them. 'Why, that would be great. Thanks. You look through here and then press right here.'

Olivia handed her precious camera over without a qualm and ran to Nick's side. She put her arm through his as if it was the most natural thing in the world, and stood close against him, as if for warmth. For a moment Nick's face grew tense as he looked into her eyes, but then Olivia turned to smile at the camera and he, too, reluctantly turned his head.

When they reached the pub Olivia lost no time in taking that film out of the camera, even though she hadn't yet finished the reel; she wanted to be sure that no accident would happen to make her lose that shot.

The pub was shut, so instead they bought a French loaf, butter, and a lump of cheese, which they ate in the chopper and washed down with cans of drink. It was a crazy, uncomfortable kind of picnic, but because of that it was fun, too. Filled with a sudden surge of adrenalin, Olivia did her impression of Katharine Hepburn and Humphrey Bogart, pretending that they'd got marooned in a helicopter instead of *The African Queen*.

It made Nick grin and, after an inward struggle, he joined in, but mimicking Laurel and Hardy instead. It was the kind of witty, spontaneous funning that they'd often shared when they were together back in New York, when they had been close in mind as well as in body, striking sparks off each other mentally as well as sexually. Inevitably it brought back memories, all of them good. Her eyes alight, laughing, Olivia tried desperately not to say, 'Do you remember?' But Nick must have been thinking it too, because he stopped laughing quite suddenly and turned away, a lost, unhappy look in his eyes.

Reaching out, Olivia put her hand over his. 'We had such good times,' she said softly.

'Yes.' Nick nodded, his face softening.

'Please—won't you tell me what's the matter?' she pleaded.

His hands doubled into fists. 'I can't.' He looked into her eyes. 'Don't ask me again, Olivia.'

It was a statement, a question, and a plea. He waited, and she knew she had no alternative but to give him the assurance he wanted. 'No, all right,' she agreed with deep reluctance.

That afternoon she had arranged to visit another castle a little further south but still on the coast, but this one, Bamburgh, was very different. Again she had to walk quite a way to reach it, but Nick didn't come with her this time. Olivia didn't mind so much because the castle was full of the most beautiful things: armour, porcelain, jade, paintings; she spent much longer than she'd intended looking round, and then had to hurry back to the village and the field where Nick waited. But on the way she passed the little Grace Darling museum, and just had to go inside to see what it was all about. The main feature was a big, heavy-looking rowing-boat which the twenty-three-year-old Grace Darling had helped her father, the local lighthouse-keeper, to row through through wild seas to rescue the crew of a ship driven on to the rocks in 1838. The story caught at her imagination as it had caught at that of Grace's contemporaries, who had turned her into a national heroine.

'Olivia.'

She turned from the showcase she was poring over. 'Oh, hi, Nick.'

'I thought I'd find you in here. You're already an hour later than you said you'd be.'

'I didn't know I was going to find this place. And the castle was full of fascinating things,' she explained excusably.

He didn't stop to tell her off, just said sharply, 'We've got to get going. The weather is closing in.'

They went out into the street and she saw that the sun had gone completely, the air smelt cold and damp and there were swirls of mist rising. Olivia hesitated. 'Will it be all right to go back? Perhaps we ought to stay here tonight and go back tomorrow?'

'No way,' Nick said firmly. 'Come on, let's get going.'

It had been an innocent enough suggestion, but Nick had obviously taken it the wrong way, perhaps even seeing her tardiness as a ploy to make it necessary for them to stay at a hotel together. Olivia realised this, belatedly, and almost wished she had, but Nick was in no mood, and hurried her along to the chopper. He shooed off the usual group of people who had come to have a look, and took off immediately.

The mist was below them, on the ground, but the sky overhead was almost as dark as night. Leaving off her head-set, Olivia concentrated on speaking her impressions into her microcassette recorder, her eyes half closed, unaware of her surroundings. She was still concentrating hard when Nick reached over and tapped her on the knee to attract her attention. He pointed to the headset and she put it on.

'I'm going down to re-fuel.'

He landed at a small airfield, and Olivia climbed out of the chopper after him. 'Is there somewhere we can get a drink?'

'Sorry, there's no time. The fog is spreading south and I need to keep ahead of it.'

But Nick not only had to fly south but also westwards, and as they travelled towards Stratford the mist gradually enveloped the ground below them. Olivia sat quietly, not exactly unconcerned but not afraid either. She knew Nick was a good pilot so she let him concentrate on flying by his instruments, and listened as he spoke on the radio to men at stations on the ground who were guiding them home.

As they neared Harnbury he pressed another button on the radio and they heard Bill Fairford's voice in relieved answer. 'About time you checked in, boss. I was just going to go home and have my supper.'

Nick grinned. 'We're almost there. Turn the lights on, will you, Bill?'

Almost immediately a group of powerful floodlights bit through the fog a couple of miles or so over to the west. Olivia pointed excitedly and Nick nodded.

'Do you see them, boss?'

'We see them, Bill. Be with you in a couple of minutes. You should be able to hear us soon.'

'I'll go outside and wait. Over and out.'

It was a strange, ghostly feeling as the 'copter descended slowly into the circle of light and then into the mist, the rotor blades sending it swirling madly about them. The ground was completely invisible and it was as if they were going down into a bottomless tunnel of grey cotton wool. But then they touched the ground as lightly as if it had been broad daylight, and Nick switched off the engine, letting the silence encompass them. He turned to Olivia. 'Sorry about that. You were very brave. I hope you weren't too frightened.'

Olivia took off her head-set. 'I wasn't brave because I wasn't frightened. I trust you.'

Nick seemed about to say something, but Bill came over and opened her door. 'You all right, Olivia?'

'Sure. Fine.' He helped her out and she was amazed at how thick the fog had become. He had turned off the big floodlights and there were only the lamps by the hangars and that from the windows of the offices to penetrate the enveloping murky darkness. 'This way,' Bill said, taking her arm to guide her to the office building.

Nick followed, bringing her camera-bag. 'Have the others got back safely?' he asked Bill.

'Been back for hours and gone home before it got thick. Jane, too. The roads are really bad,' he added with relish. 'Traffic jams for miles on all the major roads and approaches into the towns. There was a bulletin on the radio telling people not to drive, said it would be suicidal.'

Nick frowned. 'Olivia has to get to Stratford.'

'Not tonight she won't. There was a pile-up on the A439 about an hour ago, and the tail-back is so long that people are just abandoning their cars and walking.'

'The A439? That's the road from here to Stratford, isn't it?' Olivia asked.

'Yes,' Bill nodded. 'Well, I'm off home myself now you're back safely.'

'But how are you going to get home?' Olivia exclaimed. 'Surely you're not going to risk driving after all you've said?'

'No, I only live in the village. I always walk—and I could find my way blindfold. See you tomorrow, then, boss.'

'Wait a minute, Bill.' Nick put out a hand to stop him. 'If Olivia can't get back to Stratford she'll need somewhere to stay. Could your wife put her up for the night?'

The elder man shook his head regretfully. 'Sorry I can't help, but we've got our daughter and her kiddies staying with us. The little boy's even sleeping on the couch.'

Nick nodded and stepped back. 'Thanks, anyway. And thanks for being here to guide us in, Bill.'

A tense silence fell after Bill left. To break it Olivia said, 'I'm longing for a hot drink. Would you like a coffee?'

'Yes. Please.'

She went into the kitchen to make it, and Nick went outside, to see for himself just how bad it was, presumably. When Olivia came from the kitchen with two mugs of coffee he was on the phone, getting an up-to-date weather report. When he'd finished his face looked grim. 'I'm afraid Bill was right; there's no way you're going to be able to drive home in this.'

'Maybe it will clear in a couple of hours.'

Nick shook his head. 'No, it's set in for the night.'

'A famous British fog!' Olivia exclaimed brightly. 'What is it you call them—super somethings?'

'What?' Nick's brows drew into a frown, then cleared as he gave a small grin. 'I think you mean pea-soupers. We don't have them so much nowadays; it's just our luck that it's happened today.' He frowned again and said tersely, 'I can probably make it home, but I don't know what to do about—'

'Don't worry about me,' Olivia broke in, her chin rising. 'I can push a couple of armchairs together in the rest-room and sleep on those. Just so long as there's something to eat. I'm starving.'

They went into the kitchen to look, but could only find some cans of non-alcoholic beer in the fridge and a couple of chocolate bars in a cupboard. Nick swung the door of the cupboard shut in anger. 'There ought to be some emergency food here.'

'Don't worry,' Olivia said shortly. 'I'll manage perfectly well.' She went into the rest-room and began to drag the chairs together.

Nick stood in the doorway for a moment, his face grim. 'Leave that,' he ordered. And added with deep reluctance, 'You'd better come home with me.'

'No, thanks. I'll be fine here.'

'No, you won't; the heating goes off at night and you'll be cold and hungry.'

'I wouldn't dream of putting you out,' Olivia answered with formal hostility, aligning the chairs.

'You can't stay here.'

'Yes, I darn well can!' She went over to draw the curtains across the windows, but Nick came over and caught her arm, swinging her round. Olivia faced him in hurt anger. 'You don't want me to go with you; you've made that clear enough.'

'No, I don't!' Nick admitted fiercely. 'But you can't stay here.'

She gave a scornful laugh. 'What are you afraid of— that I'll attack you or something?' His grip on her arm tightened so sharply that Olivia winced, but she immediately felt guilty when she saw the sudden bleakness in his eyes. 'I'm—I'm sorry,' she muttered, and bit her lip.

'There are parts of my life I would have preferred to keep private,' he told her harshly. Letting her go, Nick stepped away and gave a mirthless laugh. 'But it seems there's no help for it.' Picking up his coffee, he drank it down, then, in control of himself again, said curtly, 'We'd better get going.'

Using a strong torch to light their way, they set off through the fog, Nick taking the long way round by the road and up to the big stone entrance. He unlocked the gates with a key, but Olivia made no comment as he held one open for her to walk through. And she stayed silent as they walked down the long driveway, their footsteps echoing hollowly in the fog. They reached the house more

quickly than she had done by the lower road when she'd
had to negotiate all the fallen trees, but she could see little of it in the foggy darkness. A light burned in the entrance porch but there were none at the windows, and no
one came forward to welcome them when Nick unlocked the door and ushered her in.

He led her into a kind of hallway, said, 'Wait a minute,' and went to switch on more lights.

The place smelt of age and dust and damp, so that
Olivia didn't know what to expect. But she gaped in
astonishment as the lights of a great hanging chandelier
revealed a wide and beautiful carved oak staircase, portraits and tapestries on the walls, an age-old chest against
the panelling.

'This way.'

Hastily she followed Nick as he went through a door
on the left. He switched on more lights, and she found
herself in a huge dining hall two storeys high. A great
carved marble fireplace was in the centre of the long wall
to her right, and down the length of the middle of the hall
ran an immense refectory table with a couple of dozen
high-backed chairs set on either side. But it was to the far
end of the room that her eyes were drawn, to an exqui-
sitely carved oak screen that stretched the width of the
room and so high that it formed a gallery for the second
storey. Above it there was an ornate plaster-work ceiling, its colours hidden by masses of cobwebs that hung
down so low she could almost reach them.

Nick had walked on, but Olivia stood in the middle of
the room and stared round until her eyes almost fell out.

'This way,' Nick said again, but she couldn't move.

'My God, Nick, do you really live in this place?'

'Yes.' His reply was short. 'Are you coming?'

Dragging her gaze away, Olivia hurried to join him, her eyes searching his face, but he said nothing more until they reached a smaller room, the one that she'd seen when she'd looked through the windows. Nick drew the curtains and knelt to light the fire, putting on screwed-up newspaper and thin sticks, then adding logs when it caught. He did it so skilfully that she knew it must be an everyday task, and guessed that this was his sitting-room, the place with the single armchair, where he spent his lonely evenings.

He straightened up and saw she was still standing. 'Sit down and get warm; I'll go and light a fire in one of the bedrooms for you.'

'Can I help?'

Nick hesitated, then shrugged. 'All right, you can carry some logs.'

He took her into a surprisingly small kitchen, where an Aga cooker gave out a welcome heat. Beside it was stacked a pile of neatly sawn logs. Each carrying an armful, he led the way up a small narrow staircase to an upper corridor, to a room that was shrouded in dust-covers. Nick pulled some of them off to reveal a four-poster bed with pretty, feminine hangings. 'It's a bit dusty in here, I'm afraid, but it isn't damp. And there's a bathroom through that door.' He indicated a door so well concealed in the wall that Olivia hadn't noticed it. He lit the fire while she explored the bathroom, falling in love with the antique bath on ornate metal feet, and the pretty, flower-bedecked wash-basin and toilet.

There were so many questions she longed to ask, but was wise enough to wait. This house, she guessed, must have a great deal to do with why Nick had changed, and she remembered that she'd promised not to ask him about that again. When the fire was going well, Nick found some sheets and a duvet, and they made up the bed between them; then they went back to the kitchen and Nick looked in the freezer. 'There should be something here we can eat.'

'Why don't you let me look?'

This time he didn't hesitate. 'OK.'

There was lots of food, but it was the sort of food a man on his own would have in stock: ready-meals and packets of frozen vegetables. Using them, and some fresh stuff she found in the fridge, Olivia managed to put together a halfway decent meal which they carried through to the sitting-room. Nick took a bottle of white wine from a small wine-rack in the corner.

'Don't you have a cellar?' Olivia commented.

'A huge one—but it's too far to go just for a bottle of wine.'

They sat down to eat, and after a few minutes Nick raised a sardonic eyebrow. 'Are you sulking?'

'I don't sulk—you should know that,' she shot back.

'In that case you're behaving very unnaturally. You must be dying of curiosity about this house, and yet you haven't asked me one question about it.'

'I promised not to.'

He frowned for a moment. 'But that was about—' Nick broke off as he saw her eyes widen. 'What do you want to know?' he said quickly.

'Do you live in this huge place alone?'

'Yes.'

A typically unhelpful masculine answer. 'Are you looking after the place for the owner? Are you some kind of caretaker?'

'I suppose you could call me that,' Nick agreed, again on a sardonic note. 'A caretaker for posterity.'

'Posterity? I don't understand.'

Nick picked up their soup plates and collected the next course from a heated trolley. When he sat down again he said, 'The house is mine.'

'Yours?' Olivia stared at him in stupefied amazement.

Leaning forward, Nick pushed her dropped jaw back up and closed her mouth. 'Yes. I inherited it from my father.'

Recovering a little, Olivia said, 'But you never said anything about your father owning a place like this when we—when you were working for the airline.'

'He didn't own it then. It belonged to my great-uncle, who had been more or less a recluse for twenty years. He just lived in a couple of rooms and let the rest deteriorate—as I'm doing,' he added with a grim smile.

'And when your great-uncle died your father inherited it?'

'Yes, and had to pay a large inheritance tax. And then, of course, my father was killed just a few months later so that I had to pay another inheritance tax on the place. I had just enough left to set up the helicopter business.'

'So there was no money to spend on the house?'

'No.' He gave an expressive wave of his hand. 'As you see.'

'But it must be full of valuable things.'

'Not as much as you think. My family were supposed to have come over with the conqueror, and flourished for a while, but then the main branch died out and those left were reduced to being not much more than farmers and lords of the manor until they got rich again by selling wool. So they built this house to establish their rediscovered status, but unfortunately the wool industry collapsed and they were unable to buy enough land to maintain the house. A place of this size needs plenty of land—forestry and farms—to provide the money to support it. So there was never enough money to repair it properly, to replace the furniture, or put in modern amenities.'

'So nearly everything in the house is original to when it was built?'

'Yes. Original—but threadbare. And I'd like to keep it that way if I can.' He paused, searching for words. 'I feel a kind of responsibility towards all my ancestors; I don't think they'd approve if I sold off the heart of the house to maintain the shell.'

Olivia looked up at the portraits on the walls, wondering if the spirits of these people in their powdered wigs and satin dresses were here, watching and listening to them. But she felt no chill of coldness down her spine, only the warmth of the fire and the aged beauty of the room. 'Are you going to keep it, then?'

'I'd like to—for a while.' His eyes shadowed. 'But I don't see much hope. I'll probably end up giving it to the National Trust, if they'll take it. They usually like a large endowment to go with a house when they take one over.'

'I guess you don't even have much time to spend here?'

'If I have a few hours to spare I hack away at the garden or do some work in the house. And I have a woman from the village who comes in four mornings a week to clean the rooms I use and do what she can.'

'Have you thought of opening it to the public?'

'I do on some summer weekends, but to do it regularly you'd need lavatories and a car park and guides—so many things that it would take years to recoup your investment.'

'Can't you get grants and things to help?'

'Yes, if you're willing to sell your soul to local government bureaucracy.'

'Will you show me round?'

Nick smiled. 'I wondered when you'd get round to that. Yes, all right. Are you going to start eating that?' he added, pointing. 'I thought you said you were starving.'

Olivia looked down at her untouched plate and laughed. 'I was so amazed at you really owning this place that I completely forgot about the food.'

'That must be a first, then,' Nick commented.

Her eyes softened. 'No, I think there have been other times that I've been distracted since we met.'

But that was getting on to dangerous ground and Nick quickly changed the subject.

After their meal he took Olivia on a slow tour round the house. Most of the rooms had their furniture swathed in dust-sheets that didn't look to have been moved for years, so that clouds of throat-catching dust floated in the air whenever Nick lifted one off to show her a beautifully carved day-bed or an oak chair black with age. There was a whole set of priceless porcelain in a display cupboard but holes in the oak floorboards, a beautiful portrait by a renowned painter but a large crack in the ornate ceiling, the ticking of a beautiful long-case clock but the scuttle of mice along the library shelves.

They came to a stop in a long, shadowed picture gallery on the first floor, its walls smelling of mustiness, and Olivia looked around her. 'This place,' she announced firmly, 'needs some tender, loving care.'

Nick gave her a wary look. 'I don't think I like the tone you said that in.'

'You can't just leave it to rot like this; something has got to be done—and done fast.' She turned a bright, excited gaze on him. 'I could write about it; it's the sort of story the Americana public would love, especially the women. Every housewife in the country would see it as a challenge, transforming a place like this, making it bright and clean again. We could offer working holidays,' she said enthusiastically. 'People could stay here for free in return for fixing the plumbing or mending the tapestries.'

Nick raised an eyebrow. 'We?'

The one word brought her devastatingly back to earth, but Olivia recovered valiantly and said, 'Sure. I'd do the organising from the American end.'

He gave a small, disbelieving smile but said, 'Have you seen enough?'

'What more is there to see?'

'Attics, cellars, a dozen or so more bedrooms, the servants' quarters, the original kitchen, the—'

'OK,' Olivia cut in. 'I get the picture. We'll save it for daylight. Do you have a phone? I ought to ring my hotel and tell them I won't be back tonight.'

'It's in my sitting-room. Think you can find your way? I'll get some more logs for the fire.'

He strode off, and Olivia followed more slowly, turning out the lights, stopping to look at things she hadn't noticed before. Reaching the foot of the stairs, she confidently turned in what she thought was the direction of the sitting-room—and of course got hopelessly lost. Ever a romantic, Olivia thought she ought to be carrying a branched candlestick that flickered in the draught and finally blew out and left her alone in the dark in the strange, haunted house. Instead she flicked on electric lights and felt no fear as she looked in empty rooms and yelled, 'Nick! Hey, I'm lost.'

After about ten minutes he came to find her and took her back to the sitting-room. Olivia called the hotel and afterwards Nick suggested they watch the television for a while so that they could find out about the extent of the bad weather on the news. 'If it keeps up like this we'll lose all our work tomorrow,' he said grimly.'

'Does it often happen? she asked, looking across at him. He had brought in another armchair and set it at the other side of the fire.

'Too often, in the winter. You can't take learners up if the weather is at all bad. And it costs money to have the choppers and pilots just sitting around waiting for the weather to improve.'

To divert him, Olivia said, 'I think I'd like to learn.'

Nick gave a lazy grin. 'Got hooked, have you? I suppose you think it looks easy.'

'I think you make it look easy, but I'm sure it's not.'

'Well, that makes a change; most pupils think if they can drive a car they can fly a chopper.'

Olivia almost asked, 'Will you teach me?' but remembered that she had very little time left. Her face shadowed and she looked down into the fire at the spurting flames that came from the sweet-smelling applewood logs.

A silence fell between them, but after a couple of minutes Nick said, 'The next programme looks quite interesting; let's watch it, shall we?' and he turned up the sound.

It wasn't interesting; it was a deadly boring programme about gravity waves. But Olivia's eyes remained fixed on the screen although she let her mind wander almost at once. Finding out that Nick owned this magnificent house had been a shock, and for a while she'd thought that inheriting it was the reason for the change in him. OK, he'd also inherited a great many financial worries with it, but surely that hadn't been enough to change his whole attitude, especially his attitude to her. Was he afraid that she would want him just for his house? But that was a stupid idea; she'd been crazy about him long before that, as Nick very well knew. Back at his office Nick had said that he didn't want to bring her here, that there were things he wanted to keep private. Presumably he meant the house. And if he didn't want her to write about it then she wouldn't, of course. But she couldn't help thinking there was more to it than that. She had got closer to Nick tonight, but he was still holding back; she hadn't got close enough.

After the programme Olivia insisted on taking the plates back to the kitchen and washing them up. She also wiped down all the work surfaces—not that they really needed it because Nick's cleaning woman kept the room neat, but she didn't want to just sit and pretend to watch television any more.

Going back to the sitting-room, she stood in the doorway and said, 'It's been a long day. I guess I'll go to my room. Is there hot water for a bath?'

'That's one thing I do have.' Nick switched off the television set and got to his feet. 'I'd better show you the way in case you get lost again.'

They climbed the creaking back stairs and walked along the corridor to her door. Olivia hesitated. 'Where's your room—just in case there's a fire or something?'

Nick visibly hesitated, then pointed two doors back along the corridor towards the staircase. 'In there. If you scream loud enough I'll probably hear you.'

'Well, that's comforting. Goodnight.'

The room was warm now, the flames giving a welcoming glow to the room. Olivia switched on a couple of lamps, one of which immediately popped and went out again, but she preferred the firelight anyway. As Nick had promised, the water was beautifully hot, and he'd put out soap, a new toothbrush and toothpaste for her. And when she went back into the bedroom after drying herself she found a pair of his pyjamas on the bed. Which was a double surprise because she'd never known him to wear pyjamas; in New York he'd always worn boxer shorts if he'd worn anything at all. She put them on and laughed at her reflection in the mirror; she looked like a child dressed up in adult clothes. As she watched, the trousers, that fastened with a button at the waist, gradually slid off her slim hips and fell to her feet. Olivia stepped out of them, deciding to make do with just the jacket.

Thrilled at the thought of sleeping in a four-poster, Olivia climbed into the high bed, and was touched to find that Nick had put a hot-water bottle into it for her. But even so the sheets felt cool for a while, keeping her awake even if she'd wanted to sleep. But she was too tense, too aware of Nick being only a couple of rooms away. She turned restlessly, not used to the soft, down-filled mattress, but knew it was more than that. Her libido—or, in other words, good old-fashioned sexual desire—was giving her hell. Olivia thought of the times when they'd made love back in the States, of Nick's eagerness, of his overwhelming need for her. Surely he couldn't have changed so completely that he had no interest in sex any more? But no, of course he hadn't; Olivia thought of the one kiss he'd given her since she'd been here and knew that fundamentally he was the same.

It was no good; she just couldn't sleep. Olivia sat up in the big bed. Is Nick feeling like this? she wondered. Will he come to me? Time passed and the fire died down, but not the fire that grew deep inside her. A strange kind of anger at Nick's rejection filled her heart. He'd said that any woman would do for him; well, she was a woman, wasn't she?

Throwing back the covers, Olivia got out of bed and went quickly to the door, carried there by the force of anger. The corridor was in darkness but she could see well enough to find her way to Nick's door. There was no lock on it, just as there was none of hers. Taking a deep breath, Olivia turned the handle and slipped inside.

CHAPTER EIGHT

THE lamp beside Nick's bed was still alight and there was an open book in his slack hand; he must have fallen asleep while he was reading. By its light Olivia crept over to his bed. Carefully she took the book from him and put it on the bedside table. She stood for a long moment looking down at him, her heart full of love, her body urgent with longing. He was going to be awfully mad at her, she supposed, but she hoped that her being here, offering herself to him, would awaken his desire and kill his anger.

As she watched he moved restlessly and began to mutter in his sleep. A bad dream, or was he, too, torn by desire, even though he was asleep? Olivia reached up to undo the buttons of her pyjama jacket, but paused when Nick flung his arms out of bed and pushed down the duvet as if he was terribly hot. His chest was bare and in the dim light she thought she could see strange splodges of colour running across his chest and arms. Puzzled, she leaned closer, then gave a gasp of horror. They were scars. The red, contused marks of terrible burns. Swaying with shock, unable to think, Olivia turned to leave but stumbled against the table and sent the book and a glass crashing to the floor.

Immediately Nick woke and saw her. He sat up, pulling the duvet over him, but then saw by Olivia's stunned, horrified face that he was too late. 'What the hell are you doing here?' he demanded savagely.

'Nick, oh, God, Nick, your poor chest.' Olivia put her hands up to her face, trembling violently.

Jumping out of bed, Nick strode over to her. Getting hold of her arms, he yanked them violently down. 'You just couldn't take no for an answer, could you? Could you, you little bitch?' He shook her forcefully. 'All right, well now you know why I've changed so much, why I didn't want you near me.' He gave a sobbing kind of groan. 'And you've reacted in exactly the way I expected you to. You're sickened by what you've seen.'

'No! No, that isn't true.' Olivia tried to speak but he was still shaking her, his face tormented.

'Why couldn't you keep away? Why couldn't you just go away and leave me alone?' Furiously he pushed her away from him.

Olivia almost fell, but regained her balance and ran to him. 'Why didn't you tell me? Was it the plane crash? Oh, Nick, my poor darling.'

'Yes, that's right—poor Nick. That's what I'll always be to you now, won't I? A thing of horror. A burnt—'

'Don't!' Olivia tried to put her hand over his mouth but he wrenched it away. 'Oh, Nick, don't, please.'

'I ought to really shock you,' he said fiercely, his lips drawn back in a snarl. 'I ought to tell you about the rest of what happened to me. That would really turn you off, really make you sick.' He gave a sudden savage laugh that was worse than any anger. 'Did you come in here for sex? Is that what you wanted? Well, you've come to the wrong place, to the wrong man! And now you've seen yourself, you can damn well get out!'

Grabbing her, Nick half carried, half dragged her to the door and flung it open. Olivia tried to resist, tears running down her cheeks, trying to speak through her sobs. 'No, Nick, let me stay. Talk to me. I don't care about it. It doesn't make any difference.'

But Nick pushed her violently out into the corridor. 'Well, it damn well does to me!' he yelled, and slammed the door.

Olivia ended up against the far wall, but immediately went back and beat on the door. 'Nick, please let me in. You've got it all wrong.' But she heard him dragging something across in front of the door.

'Go away, Olivia. Just go away and leave me alone.'

She called his name a couple more times but knew that it was no good. Slowly she went back to her own room, feeling numb with shock. Her heart was filled with anguish at the terrible pain he must have gone through. If only she had been with him, had been able to help him bear the pain of his injuries. They, and the grief over his father's death, must have been an almost impossible burden to bear. But Nick was strong and he had recovered, except for this terrible masochistic pride that had made him so angry with her.

Reaction set in, and she began to shiver as if she was very cold, her whole body trembling. Quickly Olivia climbed back into bed, but sat up, pulling the covers up to her chin as she leaned back against the carved headboard. She tried to think, but her mind kept going off at tangents. He'll never forgive me for this, was the uppermost thought. She'd made such a mess of things, walking in on him like that, but how could she possibly have known? I should have waited, Olivia told herself with fierce self-reproach. I should have waited until he told me himself. But the fool of a man had such pride that he might never have told her, would have let her go back to America without her ever knowing why he was keeping her at a distance, treating her as if he no longer loved her.

Forcing her brain to work, she tried to think it through, realising it *must* have been the plane crash in which he'd sustained such terrible injuries. There had been that long gap when he hadn't answered her letters; Nick must have been in hospital then. And when he'd found out the extent of his injuries he had written that terrible letter breaking up their relationship. But just for a few scars? Did he really think she'd give up loving him because of that? If so, he couldn't think much of her character or place much faith in her love for him. But then Olivia remembered what Nick had shouted at her in his fury: that other, worse things had happened to him. She shivered again, realising she probably still didn't know the half of it. Oh, Nick. She tried to send her love to comfort him, willing him to sense it and to come to her.

Olivia stayed awake the whole night, lonely and miserable as she knew Nick must be. But he didn't come to her room, and she hadn't really expected him to. It had been such a long day, and she felt terribly, oppressively tired, but didn't attempt to sleep, knew that she couldn't even if she tried. Her mind kept going round in circles, trying to think what was best to do, how to handle it. One thing was for sure; she wasn't going tamely back to the States. Nick had been so careful not to let her know anything about what had happened to him that her seeing his scars must have been a great emotional shock. Olivia could understand that. And she guessed that his reaction would be to behave even more coldly and cruelly towards her in an attempt to make her hate him and go home. Well, she wasn't going to fall for that one either, she thought with steely determination. Now she knew why he was acting like this she could easily find the strength and courage to take it.

She closed her eyes tiredly, her head aching. Now she knew why Nick had seemed so mixed up, hating her one moment, then showing that he cared the next. The crazy idiot; he must have longed to be close to her and yet afraid that she would be repulsed by his scars. And rather than face that, or have her stay with him out of pity, he had tried to convince her that he no longer loved her. But thankfully she had been stubborn enough to stay, encouraged by the few glimpses of his real emotions underneath the cold indifference. Olivia sighed; she certainly hadn't helped any when she'd let Nick see her horror tonight—but it had been horror at the pain he must have gone through, not at his poor scarred body.

Turning restlessly, she decided that poor was entirely the wrong word. Certainly not one that could be applied to Nick, whatever his injuries. But if it was pity he was afraid of, then OK, fine—he sure as hell wouldn't get any from her! Olivia grew still, the idea filling her mind. He not only wouldn't get any pity, he'd get exactly the opposite. She thought about it feverishly, a glimmer of hope filling her heart. It would mean belittling his injuries and being scornful of his over-sensitivity, but it was the only way she could see out of the problem. It would be hard, she thought grimly, especially now that he'd seen how horrified she'd been. But she'd do it somehow; she just *had* to. There seemed to be no other way, none that would overcome Nick's angry pride and give them a chance of happiness. And there was nothing to lose; nothing could be worse than the way things were between them now.

Daylight began to permeate the threadbare velvet curtains, reveal the shabby grandeur of the room. Nick also had the problem of this house on his shoulders—another immense burden that he was trying to bear alone. The proud idiot, Olivia thought, pity now banished entirely from her mind. What we need here is some energy and initiative! Getting swiftly out of bed, she had a shower, dressed, and took a notebook and pen from her bag. Impatient of the dim light, she opened the curtains—and stood entranced at the view. During the night the skies had cleared, a breeze blowing the fog out of existence. Now the sun shone on what had once been a formal garden graced with stone statues and a fountain. No water jettied from it now of course, and the garden paths were overgrown, but the basic beauty of symmetry was there, and beyond the garden parkland that fell away to the lake in the valley. She gazed for several minutes, the scene delighting her eyes, but then Olivia remembered and tore herself away to go and sit at the table and write.

When Nick came downstairs at seven-thirty he found Olivia in the kitchen, an apron tied round her waist, busily preparing breakfast. He walked into the room, his face drawn and wary, the shadows round his eyes proving that he, too, had spent a sleepless night.

Olivia gave him a quick glance, then said, 'Hi. I'm cooking you the works—what they call in the hotel "a full English breakfast", so I hope you're hungry.' He didn't answer so she told him cheerfully, 'It's about ready. Shall we sit down?'

She gestured towards the table, and Nick's eyebrows rose; Olivia had found a yellow gingham cloth, and there was a vase of daffodils that she'd picked from the garden in the centre of the table.

'Trying to cheer up the invalid?' he said with jeering masochism.

Olivia's eyebrows rose. 'I'm trying to feed myself up ready for the day ahead; I have a busy schedule lined up.'

She set the plates on the table and sat down. 'I imagine you're busy too, aren't you?' He was watching her frowningly, and she looked up. 'You don't mind if I start, do you? I want to get back to Stratford.'

Slowly he came to sit opposite her, his eyes still searching and wary. Olivia's face was clean; she'd had no make-up except lipstick with her, and there was no way she could disguise the tiredness round her eyes. 'You look as if you haven't slept,' Nick said pointedly.

'You're right, I didn't,' Olivia agreed calmly, taking him by surprise. 'And it's your fault.' She saw him stiffen, and went on, 'You'll have to make getting new curtains for that guest-room one of your first priorities; the sunlight came straight into my room at some unearthly hour this morning.'

Nick looked taken aback for only a moment, but then his face hardened. 'Are we going to pretend that nothing happened last night?'

'Nothing did.'

'I would hardly call it nothing,' he said with harsh sarcasm.

'Oh, you mean me seeing your scars. So I saw them—so what?'

'You hardly seemed to have such a casual reaction last night.'

Olivia took another bite of her breakfast and reached for the salt-cellar. 'Say, do you have any more salt? This is empty.'

'I've no idea.'

'Remember to put some on your shopping list. What were you saying? Oh, yes, my reactions last night.' She shrugged. 'Sure, I was shocked. Who wouldn't be? It must have been a terrible crash—I take it you got those injuries in the plane crash?' Nick nodded, not eating, his eyes intent on her every move. Olivia's heart fluttered, but she went on, 'So you were in an accident, so you were hurt; I really don't see why you're making such a big thing of it. Unfortunately accidents happen all the time. Some people get killed, some are lucky and live. You were lucky.'

'Lucky?' He flicked the word at her like a whiplash. 'Yes, I suppose I was lucky. When the plane crashed I was knocked unconscious but my father was all right, able to walk away. But he came back to get me out. My legs were broken and he had a hell of a job. The plane began to burn and I caught fire, but he stayed with me and managed to drag me away. And when it finally exploded he covered me with his own body and was killed. So yes, I was lucky that I'm left crippled and scarred. Lucky that my father is dead and I'm not!'

He was glaring at her, his eyes savage, his hands gripping the table. Olivia stared at him, trying to fight down all the love and pity, the overwhelming feminine need to offer comfort. Instead she banged her knife down on the table and said furiously, 'Yes, you damn well *are* lucky! You're alive, aren't you? And of course your father came back and got you out. Do you really believe he would have stood by and watched you burn while there was even the faintest chance of saving you? He was your father! He loved you. He did what any parent would instinctively do. What you would have done if it had been your child in danger. And he gave his life for yours so that you could enjoy your life, not sit around feeling sorry for yourself all the time.'

Nick stood up angrily. 'I don't feel sorry for myself!'

'Of course you do. Shutting yourself away in this house, keeping me at arm's length in case I saw your scars. Hell, what are a few scars and a limp? You're not blind, are you! You're not a paraplegic stuck in a wheel-chair? If you ask me, Nick you're just a self-pitying coward.' She threw the words at him, deliberately intending to shock.

He took a stride towards her, his eyes murderous, his hands bunched into furious fists. Olivia thought that he was going to hit her, and it took all her courage not to flinch away but to glare back at him. But then Nick's face worked convulsively, and he swung round and strode out of the room, slamming the door violently shut behind him.

Olivia took a long, shuddering breath. She pushed her plate away, giving up all pretence at eating, and put a hand up to her face. For a minute there she had been sure that Nick was going to strike her. He had been so angry! But anger, she told herself, was good. It was a positive emotion. Much better than bottling his hurt up inside and trying to pretend he was OK.

Briskly, she got to her feet and cleared up the break-fast things, then went to look for Nick. She couldn't find him anywhere, but then heard a noise outside and found him round the back of the house, chopping wood. He had his shirt off and there was sweat on his skin as he worked out his anger, swinging the axe down hard to split the logs from some great tree-trunk. Lifting the axe above his head, he caught sight of her, then swung it violently down before straightening up to face her defiantly, daring her to look at his chest, fully expecting her to show pity or revulsion.

Steeling herself, knowing this was a testing moment, Olivia walked up to him, forcing herself to keep her eyes steadily on him. 'Are you about ready to go to the heli-port? Shall we walk there together?'

He didn't answer, and Olivia licked lips suddenly gone dry. 'Something bothering you?' Nick sneered.

'Yes.' She put a hand on his arm, feeling the hardness of his muscles. 'I was remembering that time we were in Vermont and you went out to chop wood for the fire.' She smiled reminiscently. 'You chopped so much we had enough for the whole week. All those log fires.' She looked up into his eyes, her own soft and sensual as she remembered how they'd made love on the big rug in front of those fires almost every night.

Nick stared at her. 'You can think of that—*now*?'

'Of course I can. It was the happiest, most wonderful time of my life. I shall never forget it, never forget you,' she said simply.

'Olivia—' he began on a note of protest.

But she leaned forward and kissed his shoulder, ran her tongue over his salty skin. Nick shuddered convulsively, then became rigidly tense, his muscles like sprung steel. But he didn't push her away. Olivia kissed his shoulder again, raised languorous eyes to meet his, then smiled and stepped back. 'I guess this is no time to start feeling sexy. Meet you in front of the house in ten minutes.'

She left him gazing after her, the axe slack in his hands, and she didn't look back as she went into the house to collect her things.

Ten minutes later Nick was waiting for her in the hall, dressed, ready for work. He locked up the house and they began to walk up the main driveway. At the bend Olivia paused to look back. 'It's so beautiful,' she sighed. 'Tell me about its history.'

His voice was reluctant at first, but it was a safe subject and after a while Nick loosened up to tell her the house's story, which was also his family's history, of course.

'And is it in the library there that you have your family tree—the one that goes back to 1066?' Olivia enquired.

'Yes, it's shut away in a drawer.'

'I'd love to see it some time.'

It was an impulsive, sincere remark, but it brought the whole question of the future back to their minds. Nick's stride lengthened and he made a non-committal reply. Olivia talked of other things, determined to try to keep the conversation, the atmosphere, as normal as possible, not to let a tense silence arise between them. When they reached the heliport Bill Fairford was already there. He strolled out of the hangar when he heard them, and didn't attempt to hide a knowing grin when he saw their sleepless faces.

'What's so funny?' Nick snapped.

'Just pleased that the fog has lifted, boss,' Bill got out smartly, the smile disappearing fast.

They separated, Nick walking towards the office building, Olivia to her car. 'Bye, Nick, see you tomorrow,' she called out.

He hesitated in his stride, but said nothing and continued on his way.

When Olivia got back to the hotel and went to get her key from the desk the receptionist also handed her several letters. Taking them up to her room, she put a 'Do not Disturb' sign on the door and dropped the letters on the bed until she'd taken a shower, brushed her hair and put on a nightgown. Then she helped herself to an orange juice from the fridge and sat cross-legged on the bed to open them. The first was a fax from her editor, congratulating her on the work she'd already sent in and asking her to do follow-ups on a couple of the articles. 'Subjects popular Stateside,' she read. 'Stay over longer if you need to.' Which was nice, and definitely improved the day.

A second letter was from a close friend, Christina, the one she mostly went to concerts and the theatre with, and who was getting a divorce, saying that she and her husband had decided to try living together again. Which was also good news, as Olivia had been convinced that they should never have separated in the first place. And a third envelope with a local postmark contained two tickets for the first night of a new production of *Measure for Measure* at the Swan Theatre that Thursday, with the manager's compliments.

There were a couple of other letters, forwarded to her by a neighbour, but nothing of any importance. Slipping into bed, Olivia lay back on the pillow, thinking about New York, something she had very seldom done since she'd been in England. With some surprise she realised that she had missed the Big Apple hardly at all. There was so much to do here, so much history and visual beauty contained in this small corner of a tiny country. Although she had no close family back home she had plenty of friends, like Christina—most of them young divorcees and career women like herself, women without a permanent man, but they had all faded into the background when Nick was so close. Now, Olivia tried to think objectively about what she wanted out of life.

It took less than a second to know that it was Nick, now and always. It would mean having to give up her career, her country, everything, but Nick desperately needed her even if his stubborn pride wouldn't admit it. When she'd come to England it had been with the idea of finding him and resolving their differences so that they could get married and go back to the States to live, where she could get on with her career. An entirely selfish dream of having the best of all worlds. But life wasn't that easy. Instinctively she knew that Nick would hang on to Harnbury Hall as long as he possibly could, which—if she could beat down his defences and make him admit that he still loved her—would mean living there. Well, that was OK; she supposed she could write anywhere, and she would love living in a house that old and beautiful, and making enough money to restore the place would be a challenge she sensed she would enjoy. But giving up her whole way of life wouldn't be an easy decision.

The biggest and most immediate problem was going to be persuading Nick that they still had a future together. But at least she'd made a satisfactory start this morning. Olivia smiled to herself, and fell asleep trying to think of ways she could convince Nick that she still loved him, despite his scars.

She slept solidly for four hours, then walked into the town for lunch in the Dirty Duck, a little pub near the River Avon. She ordered a Ploughman's: a thick hunk of fresh bread, cheese, sweet pickles, lettuce and tomato, which Nick had introduced her to and which had become a favourite lunchtime snack. I'm sitting here, watching the swans of Avon opposite the Swan Theatre at Stratford-upon-Avon, she thought, and was enraptured by it. A narrow-boat, brightly painted with traditional scenes on its sides, chugged slowly by, the man at the tiller giving her a cheery wave, the swans bobbing in its wake. Another small delight.

After lunch Olivia drove to the village of Snowshill, set on one of the highest points of the Cotswolds. It was a place she'd missed before even though there was a National Trust property there. The village nestled beneath a hill, a squat-towered church in its centre with cottages set around a sloping village green. The National Trust owned the local manor. Olivia paid her money and went in, expecting to find the usual rooms of furniture, porcelain and pictures, shaded from the sun. Instead she found a distinctly odd treasure-house of a dozen different and eccentric collections. There were innumerable clocks, model ships, navigational instruments, Indonesian artefacts, children's toys, and, in one weirdly lit room, a startling display of seventeenth-century Japanese Samurai armour, arranged as a gathering of warriors with their weapons and banners, appearing out of the gloom.

Although fascinated by all the objects, Olivia felt glad to leave the house for the sunlit garden. She wandered round for a while and then sat on one of the wooden seats near a carved stone tablet. Idly she read the inscription, and found it so apposite that she repeated the words over, learning them by heart.

'Hours fly
Flowers die.
New days
New ways
Pass by.
Love stays.'

Love stays; she repeated the thought in her mind. And I'll stay. In that moment she made the most important decision of her life. No matter how long it took, she would stay in England until she browbeat Nick into admitting that he still wanted her. Perhaps not so much in the beginning, but later on, she would probably miss America and her old life terribly, but love stays, and her love for Nick was all that mattered.

That evening she rang Nick at home.

'Hi, it's Olivia,' she said brightly when he answered. 'I've decided that tomorrow I want to go to Arundel Castle and then to Brighton to see the Prince Regent's Pavilion. Can you arrange to land at those places?'

'Yes, but... Olivia, I really think...'

'What do you really think, Nick?' Olivia asked on a warning note. 'Our contract doesn't run out for another two trips.'

He was silent for a moment, and she could imagine the effort of will it was costing him not to get angry.

'Very well,' he said shortly. 'I'll make the necessary arrangements.'

'Good. Say, are you doing anything Thursday night?'

His voice was immediately wary. 'Why?'

'I need an escort. I've been given two tickets for the first night of *Measure for Measure* at The Swan. It's black tie, so—'

'No,' Nick cut in.

Olivia's voice hardened. 'It's not only black tie, Nick; you do get to wear other clothes as well. No one's going to notice that you have a couple of scars under your evening suit.'

'Damn you to hell, Olivia!' he shouted at her, and slammed down the phone.

He was still in a black mood the next morning when she turned up at the heliport. Olivia took a look at his angry eyes and immediately became brisk and business-like, and when they got in the chopper she spent most of the journey to Arundel, not far from the south coast, reading up the report on the castle in her guide books. Originally an eleventh- and twelfth-century castle, she read, rebuilt in the eighteenth century, the seat of the Duke of Norfolk. A few weeks ago she would have been in awe of dates that old; now she took them for granted. Anyway, compared to Stonehenge they were quite new.

The thought made her smile, and Nick, glancing her way, said over the intercom, on a belligerent note, 'What are you grinning like a Cheshire cat about?'

She turned to look at him. 'I was just thinking how blasé I'm getting about history and dates. Now something has to be as old as Stonehenge before it impresses me. Perhaps I'm becoming "Old Worldified".'

'Well, make the most of it,' Nick said, his jaw set stubbornly. 'Because you'll be back in the States next week.'

'Oh, didn't I tell you?' She gave him an innocent smile. 'I had a fax from my editor yesterday; he wants me to stay on to do some more articles. Hey! Watch it!' She grabbed the side of her seat as the chopper suddenly dipped.

Nick swiftly righted it, and she burst into laughter. 'What's so damn funny?' he snapped.

'Your face! Oh, Nick, you just don't know whether to be pleased or sorry.'

'It doesn't matter to me either way. After Friday our contract comes to an end and I won't be seeing you again. Ever,' he added crushingly. 'So whether you're here or in New York doesn't make any difference.'

That's what you think, Olivia thought smugly. Have you got a few surprises coming.

'Did you say something?' Nick was watching her suspiciously, obviously expecting her to argue with him.

'No, not a thing,' she replied sweetly, and smiled into his disbelieving eyes.

'And don't expect me to come to the theatre with you tomorrow.'

'Why not?' But before he could speak, 'Why don't we talk about it some other time? Could you fly over to the left a little? I want to take a shot of that beautiful house down there. Do you know what it's called?'

Nick consulted his map. 'It's Petworth House.'

'Petworth.' Olivia made a note in the book she kept to correspond with the camera films, then looked up the place in her guide book. 'A seventeenth-century house with a Grinling Gibbons room.' She wrinkled her nose in mock disdain. 'Only seventeenth-century!'

Nick's lips twitched but he quickly turned away and managed to stifle a grin. If I can make him laugh, Olivia thought, if I can convince him that life can still be fun, then I'll be halfway there.

Arundel was a few miles from the coast, and they were able to land in the grounds. Olivia received her usual warm welcome and guided tour, but Nick didn't come with her. Nor did he after they flew the few miles further towards the coast to Brighton. They had to land outside the town, but there was a cab waiting to take her into the centre to see the Royal Pavilion, the small manor house that the Prince Regent had enlarged and transformed into his seaside palace. Olivia was suitably impressed, gazing with awed eyes at the lavish, Chinese-style décor. She could imagine the Prince Regent escaping here from his mad father and the wife he couldn't bear, indulging his eccentric taste, and entertaining his mistresses and his gambling cronies.

Her guide offered to take her for a walk round the Brighton Lanes, small narrow streets famous for their antique and specialist shops. Ordinarily Olivia would have been happy to accept, but she had other things on her mind today, so she thanked him but refused, and took a cab back to the chopper.

Nick was working as usual while he waited, writing up some reports by the look of it, as he sat in the clubhouse of the small airfield where they'd landed. He looked up in surprise when she came up to him. 'You're back early.'

'Mm. Shall we go?'

Nick glanced at his watch. 'You're due some flying time; do you want to go on somewhere else?'

'No, I guess I'd rather get back.'

He looked at her with a small frown between his brows, but gathered up his papers, paid his landing fee, and they went back to the chopper. The days were lighter for longer now that it was April, and the sun was still high as they flew over the Cotswolds. 'Want me to fly around a little? You haven't seen the Churn valley yet.'

But Olivia shook her head. 'No, thanks.'

Again Nick frowned, but headed for Harnbury-on-the-Wold. There were a couple of other pilots standing by one of the choppers when they flew in. Nick went to speak to them, leaving Olivia to collect her cameras. These she loaded into the trunk of her car, then walked over to the building and into Nick's office. He saw her go, and came quickly after her. He found Olivia looking more closely at the photos on the wall.

'Is this your father?' She pointed at the elder man.

'Yes. Is there something you want?'

'He looks nice. I wish I could have known him.' Pulling up a chair, she sat down in it and put her feet up on Nick's desk.

His face tightened, knowing she was up to something. 'I asked you what you wanted,' he reminded her, going to the other side of the desk.

'I'm waiting for you to agree to go with me to the theatre tomorrow.'

'Then you're due for a long wait.'

'Why?'

'Because I have no intention of going, of course.'

'Why not?'

'For heaven's sake, Olivia! It's perfectly obvious why not.'

'Not to me it isn't.'

'Then you must be extremely dense,' he snarled. 'I have to see you because you conned me into signing a contract to fly you around, but there's no way I want to see you socially. In fact I shall be extremely pleased when Friday comes round and I never have to see you again.'

'What a rotten liar you are, Nick,' she answered equably.

His square jaw jutted forward. 'I have never been more serious about anything in my life.'

'In that case I shall have to remind you that you owe me.'

'Owe you?' He blinked in surprise. 'For what?'

'I'd bought two tickets for a concert at the Met that time you decided to do your big "I don't break up marriages!" act and go back to England. I lost good money on those.'

'If you think a thing like that is—'

'And of course you also owe me for something else.' Olivia lifted her head to hold his eyes. 'You owe me for not answering my letters when you knew how much I loved you and needed you. You owe me for not letting me know that you'd been in the plane crash and were hurt, that you were in hospital. You let me go through hell all those months because you were determined to go through your own private hell alone, instead of letting me be here with you where I belonged. I don't think I'll ever be able to forgive you for that, Nick.'

His face had changed, grown bleak again. 'I had no right to send for you after I'd been fool—' He stopped abruptly.

'After you'd been fool enough to walk out on me?' she guessed. Olivia swung her feet down and stood up. 'But doesn't love have any rights? Doesn't a lover? OK, maybe we hadn't exchanged any vows in a church, there was no "in sickness and in health", but you knew; that I loved you, no matter what. And if you hadn't been so full of pig-headed pride you—'

She broke off and her chin came up. 'But you owe me for those months—and that's why you're going to put on your black tie and take me to that play tomorrow.' She walked to the door, then turned back to look at him as he still stood at his desk, his hands resting on it, his stern profile towards her. 'I'll meet you in the foyer of the theatre at six-thirty tomorrow evening.' He didn't speak, and she smiled a little grimly. 'So long, Nick. Be seeing you.'

That evening Olivia spent a couple of hours working out how much money she'd got left. She had lent her flat back in New York to a friend so the rent was taken care of, and she reckoned there would still be a few thousand dollars left from her aunt's legacy once she had paid for her helicopter trips, a percentage of which she felt she could legitimately claim as expenses. There would be enough anyway for a new dress to wear to the theatre tomorrow, and for a visit to a beauty salon. So Olivia spent most of the next morning shopping, and finally chose a dress in deep rose velvet, quite figure-hugging and cut slightly off the shoulder, but with long sleeves. For once she didn't feel hungry, but made herself have a salad lunch. She also spent an hour on a sunbed to freshen up her tan, and had her hair done, having it put up but with tendrils of dark curls allowed to escape around her ears and neck. Sophisticated but not over the top.

As evening approached Olivia grew tense, wondering if Nick would come. She started getting ready much too early, but took her time, wanting to look her best. When she was dressed she added perfume—Poison, Nick's favourite, the scent he had always brought her when he'd come to New York. Still only just after six, not time to leave yet. The theatre was only ten minutes' walk away but Olivia had ordered a taxi to take her, not wanting to take a chance on the weather. She went to the window and looked out, wondering for the ten thousandth time if Nick would come, whether the moral blackmail she had unashamedly used would be enough to overcome his stubbornness.

At six-twenty the desk rang through to say that her cab had arrived. Olivia picked up her coat and clutch-purse and took the lift down to the entrance. The weather was so fine and warm that she hardly needed her coat. The cab pulled up outside the theatre almost exactly at six-thirty. Olivia went inside but Nick wasn't there. She checked in her coat and went into the ladies' cloakroom for a few minutes, her heart thumping, trying not to think of what she would do if he didn't turn up. She had banked so much on tonight. When she came out five minutes later the foyer seemed to be full of tall, broad-shouldered men in evening dress. A great many heads turned to look at her appreciatively as she made her way through the crowd, but none of them was Nick's. A waiter came to offer her a glass of wine. Olivia took it with an unsteady smile and went to stand a couple of steps up the wide staircase leading to the boxes, where she could see over people's heads.

Everyone was talking and she felt deafened by the noise, wanted to scream out to them all to shut up, shut up. The big clock in the foyer said six forty-five, and she knew he wasn't going to come. Olivia took a long drink from her glass of wine, thinking that tonight would be one time in her life when it would feel good to get drunk. The main door opened again and a small group of late-comers walked in. Behind them was a tall man with dark hair in an immaculate evening suit.

Olivia drew in her breath as Nick looked about him, searching for her. He glanced up and grew very still as their eyes met. The laughing, chattering crowd dissolved and they might have been alone. Olivia's heart filled with pride at his handsomeness, and triumph that he had come. Tonight, she thought as she gazed down at Nick. Tonight I'll seduce him.

CHAPTER NINE

MEASURE FOR MEASURE was one of the few Shakespeare plays that Olivia hadn't seen before. She'd read the play, of course, and had been looking forward to seeing it, but found that she couldn't give it the attention the production deserved. Her heart was still doing crazy somersaults and she found it difficult to transport her imagination to Vienna and to the problems of other lovers. She was too full of the wonder of being here beside Nick, feeling his shoulder against hers. Too rocked by the admiration and pride that had been in his eyes when he saw her, and which he couldn't hide.

A waiter had offered him a glass of wine, and had to speak twice before Nick tore his gaze away and took a glass. He had walked through the crowd, his eyes still for her alone, and had climbed the stair to join her. He hadn't said anything—there had been no need; he had just clinked his glass against hers in a silent toast. Then the play was announced and they had quickly finished their drinks and been gathered up by the rest of the audience as they made their way to their seats in this small, pretty theatre. They were good seats, on the front row of the box, where they could look over the wooden rail down on to the projecting apron stage with the seats set round it so that the players were almost among the audience. There was a great feeling of *déjà vu*, of being back in Elizabethan times. But Olivia didn't want to go back in time; she wanted to be here, now, with Nick beside her.

During the interval they went out on to the terrace that overlooked the river. Nick leaned against the rail, his eyes on the river, but Olivia leaned back against it so that she could see him.

'You didn't go to sleep,' she said with a smile.

'No.'

Persevering, Olivia tried, 'It's a good production, isn't it? Very well acted.'

'Yes, I suppose so,' Nick straightened up and turned to her, tension in his face. 'Olivia, I—'

Swiftly she put her fingers over his mouth, afraid that he was again going to renounce her. 'Please don't spoil tonight.'

Lifting his hand, Nick took hold of her wrist and pulled it gently down. 'I was only going to say how attractive you look. That dress is—perfect for you.'

'Wow!' Olivia gave a shaky laugh. 'Now that I didn't expect.'

Nick's brows flickered and his mouth tightened for a moment, in inner anger, Olivia thought. 'You must think me an ill-mannered brute—' he began, but again Olivia stopped him.

'I *know* what you are, what you will always be to me. Nothing can change that. Not ever.' She smiled. 'No matter how hard you try.'

'I don't deserve that, Olivia.' Nick's voice grew husky.

She laughed, her heart swelling with hope. 'Probably not, but you're stuck with it anyway.' Then not wanting to get too serious yet, she said, 'How about a drink? I'm thirsty.'

He was still as good at getting drinks as ever, shouldering his way to the bar, but when he came back Olivia was talking to the theatre manager. She went to introduce him to Nick, but it turned out that they already knew each other. 'My father used to be a keen supporter of the theatre,' Nick explained.

'Which we hope you will be, too,' the manager said. 'And I hear you've inherited Harnbury Hall; I wonder if Shakespeare ever went there—it must be about his time.'

'It's possible, I suppose,' Nick agreed.

'Have you received your invitation to take part in the Birthday Celebration procession yet?' the other man asked.

'Yes, but I'm not sure whether I'll be able to take part.'

Nick said it dismissively, and the manager took the hint and didn't press him. 'Why don't you both come to the party backstage afterwards?' he invited.

'Thanks, we'd love to,' Olivia said before Nick had a chance to refuse. They talked for a few minutes longer, but then the second half was announced and the manager excused himself.

'Was that the procession through the town they hold on Shakespeare's birthday?' Olivia enquired as she and Nick made their way back to their seats.

'Yes, that's right.'

'I've read about it. How come you got invited? I thought they only had overseas dignitaries—ambassadors and that kind of person.'

'No, the format was changed recently. Now they have local dignitaries, actors from the Royal Shakespeare Company, and artistic representatives from the EC countries. They've put the emphasis on the arts rather than the diplomatic corps. Which is as it should be, I think.'

'And they've invited you as a local representative?'

'For my father's sake, as much as anything, I suppose.'

'That's good,' Olivia said warmly. 'You should be pleased—and you should go for his sake.'

'Yes, perhaps.' Nick hesitated for a moment but whatever he was going to say was lost as the next act began.

The 'backstage' party spread on to the stage itself, some of the audience staying behind for it. The actors joined in, too, but they had taken off their costumes and their make-up and were just well-known faces. Olivia was excited to see and even to meet some of them, but told Nick that she was pleased they'd taken off their costumes. 'It would destroy the magic to see the greasepaint and realise that the jewels on the costumes were only glass.'

To her surprise Nick knew several people there, mostly men he had gone to school with locally.

'Which school?' Olivia questioned.

'The grammar school, in the town.'

She stared at him. 'But that was the school that Shakespeare went to!'

'Yes, that's right.'

'Nick, I could hit you! Why didn't you tell me?'

He looked amused. 'You didn't ask.'

'For Pete's sake!' She glowered at him and thrust out her empty glass. 'I need another drink.'

He laughed and went to get her one, threading his way through the crowd.

Olivia was standing near the back of the stage, and now she turned to look around her, seeing the theatre as the actors must see it during a performance. Although it was small, the rows of seats still looked intimidating, and

Olivia couldn't see herself ever having the courage to step on to a stage in front of crowds of people.

'Hello. I don't think we've met.'

She turned as a fair-haired, very good-looking young man came over to her. He looked vaguely familiar and she frowned a little, trying to remember. 'I'm not sure.'

'I'm with the RSC,' he supplied. 'I'm appearing at the other theatre.'

'Oh, sure, now I remember. I went there a week or so ago. It was a great production.'

'Thanks.' He gave her a charming smile. 'You're American?'

'That's right.'

'And you're an actress,' he said definitely.

'Why, no. What gives you that idea?'

With flattering gallantry—or was it just plain flattery?—he said, 'Because any girl as lovely as you must surely be an actress. You outshine every woman here.'

'I agree with you.'

Nick had come up to them, and spoke from behind her. Olivia turned and took the drink from him, looking laughingly up into his eyes. 'Do you?'

'Yes.' There was an intensity in his voice and in his eyes that made her own laughter fade as she looked at him.

'Oh,' Olivia said inadequately. Remembering, she turned to speak to the young actor again, but he had gone, lost in the crowd.

'Who was that?' Nick demanded.

'An actor. I can't remember his name. He's appearing in the other theatre.'

'Humph.'

Nick made a disparaging noise, and Olivia looked at him in disbelief. 'Why, Nick, I do believe you're jealous.'

'Nonsense,' he retorted too quickly.

'No? Then why else did you come rushing back here to stake your claim?'

She said it half jokingly, but Nick frowned. 'I have no claim in you, Olivia,' he said heavily.

Not wanting the conversation to take that kind of turn, she quickly changed the subject and, as soon as they'd finished their drinks, suggested, 'Let's go, shall we?'

There was a mist on the river as they came out of the theatre, and Olivia put up the collar of her coat, glad of its warmth.

'I'll walk you back to your hotel,' Nick offered.

'OK, thanks.'

They began to walk along, Olivia's high heels echoing on the pavement, but they'd only gone a couple of hundred yards when she stopped as if something had just occurred to her. 'Hey, I just remembered: you promised to show me your family tree.'

'I don't remember promising.'

'Sure, you did,' Olivia lied. 'Let's go look at it now. Where's your car?'

'But it's gone midnight.'

'So what? In New York nobody goes to bed before two, three in the morning.'

'Maybe I'll bring it with me to the office tomorrow and you can look at it there,' Nick temporised.

She shook her head. 'I may duck out tomorrow.'

'Not fly? But why?'

Olivia shrugged. 'I guess I won't.'

'You signed that contract you're always reminding me about; I could hold you to it.' She smiled but shook her head again. His tone becoming serious, Nick asked, 'Why not, Olivia?'

'Because...' she hesitated '... because I think I'd rather tonight be our last time together.'

There was a long pause before Nick said bleakly, 'I see.'

She gave a light smile and slipped her hand through his arm. 'So let's go see your family tree. I really don't want to miss that.'

For a moment she thought he was going to refuse, but then Nick said, 'No, OK, if that's what you want.'

'Great. I can ring for a cab to bring me back.'

'Of course not. I'll take you home.'

Luckily Nick's car was parked not far away, and on the way to Harnbury Olivia kept up a bright, mostly one-sided conversation about the play and the party, not wanting to give him an opportunity to think about changing his mind. The great gates opened electronically and they drove down the curving avenue to the house at last. Olivia gave a small sigh of relief as they entered the hall, with its now familiar smell of age.

'Do you remember the way to the library?'

'I think I'd better follow you.'

The family tree was kept in a big map chest, with wide, shallow drawers that pulled out so the maps could lie flat. 'Here it is.' Nick took a vellum sheet, wrapped in layers of tissue, from the third drawer down, and laid it carefully on a big desk under the central light. He unwrapped it to reveal the family tree, yellow with age, but still legible, the names painted in with bright colours. Nick stood beside her, reading out the names as they travelled over six hundred years.

'It stops in the seventeenth century,' Olivia remarked.

'Yes, this was done in 1618; see the date there in the corner. To hang up in here when the house was built, presumably. After that all the names were put in the family Bible. Here, I'll show you.' He went over to a beautifully carved Bible-box and heaved out the huge, brass-bound volume. The front leaves were full of names and dates of birth, marriage and death. So much history in so many different hands, the scratch of quill feathers, the flow of fountain-pen. And at the very end, almost at the bottom of a page, in Nick's firm handwriting, his father's name and the date of his death.

'There's hardly space for your marriage and your children,' Olivia said stiltedly, pointing with her finger-tip.

He closed the book abruptly, and put it away in its box, locked it with an ornate silver key. 'I'll drive you back to Stratford,' he told her shortly.

But Olivia dropped her coat on to a chair, and when he turned towards her asked huskily, 'Aren't you going to kiss me goodbye?'

The light enhanced the glow of her hair and the soft sheen of the velvet dress as it clung to the curves of her body. Her lips were parted a little, ripe for kissing, her eyes were dark and sensuous with desire, and she smelt as sweet and heady as roses in the sun.

'*Olivia*.' Nick said her name pleadingly, his voice shaking with inner torment.

Walking towards him, she put her hands on his shoulders and reached up to kiss his lips, lightly but lingeringly. Then she opened her eyes and went to step back. Nick gave a strangled groan, then said, explosively, 'No!' and suddenly made a convulsive movement and grabbed hold of her, pulling her against him as he kissed her with fierce, starved compulsion. Olivia responded ardently, making him gasp, making the world whirl around them. Her hands went to his jacket, pushing it off, and then his tie so that she could unbutton his shirt and run her hands over him. All the while she kept on kissing him, not giving him a chance to think, only to feel.

He gave a great, shuddering groan when he felt her hands on his chest, and tried to lift his head away, but she moved her hips against his and felt a surge of triumph as she felt his body begin to harden. Only then did she lower her head and kiss his throat, his chest, letting her lips caress the poor reddened scars.

'Don't! Olivia, you mustn't—'

But she found his tiny, hair-circled nipples, and caressed them with her tongue, carrying him back into sensuousness.

'Dear God, Olivia, don't do this to me.'

But she went on kissing, caressing him until he groaned again, then she straightened up to kiss his mouth and said pantingly, 'Take me to bed, Nick, take me to bed.'

'I *can't*. You don't understand.'

'Yes, I do. I do understand. Let's go to bed, my darling.'

But he caught her hands and held her away from him, his breath rasping in his throat. 'I don't want your pity, Olivia.'

'Pity? Are you crazy? This is good, old-fashioned lust, and if you don't take me to bed this minute I'll—'

'You don't have to pretend. I know that no woman would want to—'

'For heaven's sake!' Olivia suddenly erupted into anger. 'I am getting just about sick to death of this. The only one around here who's doing any pitying is *you*. You're pitying yourself. I certainly don't!' And to prove it she grabbed his arm and sunk her teeth into it, hard.

'Hey! You wildcat.' He shook her off.

Putting her hands on her hips, Olivia glared at him. 'I thought you were a man, Nick, but you're not, you're

just yellow. Well, OK, if you want to go through life
feeling sorry for yourself, afraid to take a chance on living, then that's up to you. But as far as I'm concerned
you've had your chance—because I want a man in my
bed, not a coward!'

She yelled the last word at him and strode across the
room to pick up her coat, but as she reached out for it
Nick caught hold of her and swung her round so that she
fell against him. 'You little cat!' he said furiously. 'I'll
show you that I'm still man enough for you.'

His mouth came down on hers, brutal in its passion.
Olivia struggled a little to increase his anger, but then he
swung her up in his arms and was heading for his room.

They didn't get that far. Olivia bit his bare shoulder
until he cried out and threw open the door of the bedroom nearest the head of the stairs. Sweeping the dust-
sheet from the huge four-poster bed, he dropped her on
to it, and then they were rolling across its great width,
fighting, kissing, pulling at each other's clothes. His hand
found her zip and the velvet dress was thrown across the
room, followed by Nick's belt. Olivia rolled on top of
him, muttering, 'You coward,' against his lips, but at the
same time pulling off his trousers.

Then there were no more clothes between them and
Nick was on top of her. Gasping, shaking, his body
bathed in the sweat of anticipation, he put his hands on
either side of her head and looked down at her face in the
moonlight from the window. 'Olivia,' he panted. 'My
injuries—I don't know if I can.'

She kissed him fiercely. 'Well, there's sure as hell only
one way to find out.' And she arched her body towards
him.

It was she who took control that first time, taking his
body and leading him away from fear into growing ex-

citement, loving him, caressing him, not letting him think, until his body began to throb with passion and he suddenly thrust forward of his own accord. Then it was as she remembered and yet new, at one with his strength and passion, her fingers gripping his shoulders as he carried her with him into the life-meaning heights of love.

For a time afterwards they were too exhausted to speak, but then Nick turned his head and kissed her temple. 'Oh, my sweet girl,' he said brokenly. 'I thought my life was as good as over, that there was nothing left. My father dead and you lost to me. And I was so afraid I'd never be able to make love again.'

'Crazy idiot,' Olivia replied with calm satisfaction.

Nick laughed and propped himself up on his elbow, became aware of his surroundings and laughed again. 'This is the State Bed, the best in the house. I bet it hasn't seen anything like this in the last hundred years or so.'

'I think it's a very appropriate place.'

Leaning forward, he kissed her gently on the lips. 'I've an idea you planned all this.'

'Of course I did. You didn't think I was going to go tamely home, did you? You didn't stand a chance.'

'You need your head examined.'

'Only my head?' she asked pertly.

With an appreciative chuckle, Nick put his arms round her and held her against the length of his body. 'I'm the one who needs his head examined for leaving you in the first place.'

'Well, I certainly agree with that.'

'Did you really miss me?'

'Haven't I just proved it?'

His arms tightened around her. 'Oh, yes, my sweet. Thank God you did. And thank you for finding me, proving what a fool I've been,' he said in deeply felt sincerity.

Not wanting his gratitude, Olivia punched him. 'Not so much of the thanks. Having found the one guy in the world I wanted, I wasn't about to let you slip out of my hands. I'd got you nicely trained for my own benefit, not some other girl's.'

'We were always good together, weren't we?'

'Of course. Could you really doubt we'd be otherwise?'

'Not with your determination.' He lifted his hand to stroke her face. 'Olivia, my love, could you possibly—?'

'Yes,' she cut in instantly.

'Hey, you haven't heard what I was going to say yet,' Nick protested.

'If you weren't going to ask me to marry you, I'll kill you!'

He burst into rich, full-throated laughter. 'Lord, how I love you! You've made the world worth living in again.'

'It always will be.'

'Yes—now.'

'And to think how hard you tried to get rid of me, to make me go home,' she mocked.

'I'd tried so desperately to put you out of my mind. I was forcing myself to come to terms with the fact that I would always have to live alone. And then you walked into my office. I knew I should have refused to fly you, but I just couldn't resist. I told myself that I'd just have the joy of being near you for a few weeks, and then you'd go home and I'd never see you again. I even tried to make you hate me.' His face sobered again but she didn't want that. 'Olivia, I—' He gave a sudden gasp as she reached out to caress him.

'We're not going to lie here talking all night, are we?' she complained as she began to kiss him.

'Most definitely not,' he agreed as he stroked her breast. And later, thickly, 'Maybe we'd better move on to a different bed.'

'Suits me.' Lifting her up, Nick began to carry her out of the room, but slowly, kissing her as he went. Olivia gave a purr of pleasure. 'Nick, just how many bedrooms do you have in this house?'

'About sixteen, not counting the staff rooms.'

'Well, I don't want to wear you out—so how about if we use the sixteen tonight and save the staff rooms till tomorrow?'

'ARE YOU SURE I look OK?'

'You look fantastic. Don't worry,' Nick assured her as Olivia got in the car. He leaned over to kiss her, his eyes alight with love and pride.

It was only just over two weeks since they had made love on that never-to-be-forgotten night, but already Nick looked younger, less careworn. The lines of pain around his mouth were being replaced by the old laughter-lines, and there was such a spring in his step that his limp hardly showed. They hadn't gone flying the next day, had spent most of it in bed, until Olivia had gone back to her hotel, but only to pay her bill and collect her things. Then she had moved in with Nick, falling as much in love with the house as with him, and using the time he was at work to eagerly start on the library, getting rid of decades of dust, polishing and cleaning until it shone.

'I just can't get used to wearing a hat,' Olivia said now, wriggling in her seat to have another look at herself in the mirror on the car's sun-visor.

'You look beautiful. So beautiful I'm strongly tempted to stop and kiss you properly.'

'Don't you dare! I don't want my make-up mussed.'

Nick gave a mock groan. 'You'll be having headaches next.'

'That might be an idea; since you've discovered you're still capable you never stop.'

'I'm making up for lost time,' Nick returned with dignity.

Olivia laughed. 'You can say that again!'

When they reached the bend in the drive she looked back as she always did so that she could have a last glimpse of the house. Nick noticed and his face hardened a little. It was the only contention between them, the only thing they'd argued over since they'd got back together. Nick, in his happiness and gratitude, wanted to give her everything possible and so had determined to sell Harnbury Hall. 'We wouldn't be happy with the constant worry of it,' he'd insisted. 'It would take every penny I could make, and even that wouldn't be enough. No, we'll sell it and the helicopter business and go back to New York so that you can go on with your career.'

Appalled, Olivia had argued against it, loving the house, wanting to stay there. 'I don't want to go back to New York to live, I want to stay here with you.'

'But what would we do with the house, short of borrowing a small fortune to put it in repair and then opening it to the public?'

'There must be something. There has to be a way to make it pay for itself,' Olivia insisted.

'I'm not going to turn it into a country-house hotel for up-market tourists who will block the lanes with their limos,' Nick said firmly.

Olivia agreed with that whole-heartedly, but could think of nothing else. So they were at an impasse, but they'd pushed the problem aside because today was special. The morning was sunny and the countryside bursting into life, and they were on their way to Stratford to take part in Shakespeare's Birthday Procession. Olivia was wearing a cream full-skirted dress with a little jacket, and a pretty wide-brimmed straw hat decorated with flowers that Nick had picked for her from the garden. He was wearing a grey morning-suit with a top hat, and looked, in Olivia's stated opinion, a billion dollars.

Today the world had come to Stratford to honour the local boy made good. Nick and Olivia joined the other invited guests in the garden of what had been New Place—the house where Shakespeare had spent his retirement and died, which had been pulled down in 1759 by a vicar who got tired of people wanting to see round it. Olivia thought it a shame, but rather liked the eccentricity of the vicar. This morning the garden was a carpet of flowers, not only from its own flowerbeds of daffodils and tulips, but from the dozens of wreaths, posies, and bouquets that were waiting to be carried in the procession.

They were greeted by the Beadle of Stratford in his scarlet coat and gold-braided three-cornered hat, his mace in his hand. They met friends of Nick and recognised famous faces from the arts. There was a mayor in his chain of office, his Lady Mayoress by his side, there were local people and others who spoke in broken English. Everyone was dressed in his or her best: formality and colour, medals and pretty hats.

A band arrived to head the procession as it formed up, the Beadle leading the way, and as they passed through the garden they were all handed the flowers they were to carry. Olivia was given a posy of white chrysanthemums and narcissi and sprays of yellow forsythia—simple flowers for the man who must have walked among them in his own garden.

The procession left the garden and began its unhurried walk through streets lined with spectators. Accompanying them were local people dressed as characters from Shakespeare's plays, wearing costumes borrowed from the theatre. All along the route there were tall white flagpoles set into the ground, but the flags were still furled. Every time the procession reached one of the poles, one of the celebrities and a character in costume from that particular play would drop out and stand by it, waiting. Not being celebrities, Nick and Olivia stayed with the procession as it went down Waterside beside the river, where the drinkers had come out of the Dirty Duck to watch and clap, then up along Bridge Street to Henley Street to the house where Shakespeare was born.

Here they all stood in silence as the national anthem was played, then there was a huge cheer that spread through the town as every flag was unfurled simultaneously—long, brilliant yellow banners, each depicting the head of Shakespeare and the name of one of his plays or sonnets. Church bells pealed, the band played, the town was full of glorious noise. The procession closed up again as the celebrities rejoined it, but as they left Shakespeare's Birthplace children from every school in Stratford came to follow them. And at the grammar school where Shakespeare had been taught, and Nick too, the boys surged out in their straw boaters and took over the procession, mingling with the dignitaries, leading it along the rest of the way.

Olivia looked back along the cavalcade and her heart swelled; all pomp and dignity had gone, and everyone was smiling and laughing now that the children were there. What had been an international salute had now become the town's personal tribute, and all to honour not a king or a saint, but a playwright, a genius who was born and died here, but whose work would live on until the end of time.

They came to the church where Shakespeare was buried, its steeple rising up above the trees, and walked up the long avenue of stone slabs, some carved with names, like the drunken gravestones that stood among the yew trees and the Scots pines. The procession slowly went through the porch and into the church that was already bedecked with flowers on altar, and window-sills, on every pew end and around every candlestick. The building was tall and majestic, full of light that shone through the stained-glass windows. As they moved slowly forward Olivia looked at the bright, shining faces of the children and thought of all the kids back home; how they would love to come to Stratford, to see this place and go to the plays. And what a place for students who were studying Shakespeare—to actually be here and walk the streets the Bard had walked.

There was no religious service, just the simple handing over of the floral tributes. Olivia moved forward towards the chancel to hand in her flowers, and glanced up at the painted bust of Shakespeare set into the wall, with a scroll and a real white quill pen in his hand. And it was in that moment that the solution to their problem came to her. She handed over the posy, saw it laid with the others below the altar, where Shakespeare was buried, then turned to take Nick's hand and lift a glowing face to his.

'I've had the most wonderful, brilliant idea,' she said excitedly, the minute they were outside again.

'Such modesty,' he mocked, but his eyes were laughing. 'Go on; I can see you can't wait to tell me.'

'We'll turn the house into a sort of college for foreign students who want to study Shakespeare and his times. It's near enough to Stratford, and the house and furnishings are contemporary. Nothing could be more perfect. And we'll let people use the house as the setting for films; you can earn really good money from that.' She gave his arm an excited shake. 'Don't you think it's a wonderful idea?'

'Yes, but—'

'No buts,' she interrupted firmly. Taking his hand, she led him apart from the crowd, down towards the river. Earnestly she said, 'Nick, I know you're only thinking of me, but please don't sell the house or give it away. It's a part of you, as much as *I* want to be a part of you. We can make a go of it together, I just know we can. We'll make it a lived-in place again, not just a series of dimly lit rooms and a neat garden where you can't walk on the grass. It will take time, perhaps all our lives, but we can do it because we both love it enough.' She looked at him eagerly, but Nick frowned, not answering, so she said exasperatedly, 'OK, put it this way: you come with the house.'

His eyes widened and he burst into laughter. 'In that case I have no choice.'

'None at all.'

Nick leaned forward. 'Is it OK if I kiss the tip of your nose?'

She pretended to consider. 'I guess, but make it quick—I have a date.'

Putting his hands on her waist, Nick drew her to him, his eyes full of pride and tenderness as they held hers for a long moment. Then he lightly kissed her nose.

'Thank you, Miss Grant.'

'And thank *you*, Mr Vaux.'

He glanced at his watch. 'And I have a date, too.'

Taking her hand, he led her back through the church-yard, a couple of mallards from the river moving cluck-ing out of their path.

'Did you know there's a character in Shakespeare called Olivia?' he asked.

'Yes, in *Twelfth Night*.'

'And did you know there's a character called Nicholas Vaux in *Henry VIII*?'

'No! Really? You don't think...?' Olivia stopped and gazed at him in awed wonder.

'It's possible. We were around here when Shakespeare was. And the eldest son has always been called Nicho-las.' Olivia stared speechlessly, until Nick laughed and said, 'I thought you had a date?'

'What? Oh—yes. Oh, wow!'

The children, the local dignitaries, the celebrities had all gone now, down to the theatre to have lunch. But there was a small group of people standing by the porch, wait-ing.

'We thought you'd changed your minds,' Bill Fair-ford chuckled as they came up.

'Definitely not,' Nick said firmly.

He smiled at her and went into the church with an old friend of his who was to be his best man. The vicar came to greet her, and Jane, Nick's secretary, handed her an-other spray of flowers, freesias this time, before she and Bill's wife went ahead into the church. Then they heard the organ swell into triumphant sound. The vicar turned to lead the way and Olivia took Bill's arm as he escorted her down the long aisle of the flower-scented church to give her in marriage to the man she loved and thought she had lost. The man who turned to look at her with eyes so full of love that her own became misty with tears.

Through them, she repeated her vows and knelt to pray, and before her, set into the floor, was the line of simple stone slabs with the names in small, plain letters of Shakespeare's family: Susanna, his daughter; Anne, his wife. And, last of all, William Shakespeare. A great feeling of rightness, of coming home, filled Olivia's heart. She glanced up at Shakespeare's monument—and was it just a tear, or did he really wink at her?

STRATFORD-UPON-AVON — 'the romantic heart of England'

Stratford-upon-Avon lies in the gently undulating, leafy Midlands county of Warwickshire. It rests against the River Avon, on which the famous Swans of Avon can still be seen. The town is also famed for its picturesque half-timbered buildings, associated with Tudor and Jacobean times. And, of course, for its most famous son— William Shakespeare.

As the birthplace and home of the world's greatest poet and dramatist, Stratford attracts visitors from all over the world. Perhaps it's no coincidence that Shakespeare, creator of some of the most famous romantic poetry, should hail from the geographical heart of England— with its countryside abounding in beauty and history to fire the imagination.

FAMOUS LANDMARKS...

For its size, Stratford-upon-Avon has more historic buildings than any other English town. Among these are the **Holy Trinity Church** where the Shakespeare family are buried, **Shakespeare's Birthplace** and boyhood home, **New Place**, where he spent his retirement years, and **Hall's Croft**, home of his daughter Susanna. Other Shakespeare connections are the old grammar school where he was a pupil, and a little out of town are the girlhood homes of Mary Arden, Shakespeare's mother, and his wife, Anne Hathaway. Also worth a visit is **Harvard House**, the home of Katherine Rogers, mother of John Harvard, founder of the famous American university. Finally, of course, there is the **Royal Shakespeare Theatre**—one of the most famous theatres in the world— providing, along with its smaller sisters, the Swan Theatre and The Other Place, a wealth of theatrical variety.

THE ROMANTIC PAST...

As a **market town**, Stratford received its market charter in 1196, and its marketing tradition is still carried on today, with a major cattle market each Tuesday and a lively street market every Friday.

Another tradition still upheld in the town is the **Mop Fair**. An annual statute fair of very ancient foundation transforms the town centre every October 12th. This is a lively occasion with country dancing and singing, stalls, and funfair rides. In past centuries, 'the Mop' was a hiring fair, where servants would gather to offer their services. They would wear or carry something to indicate their trade, such as whipcord in a lapel, or, of course, a mop. Twelve days later, the Runaway Mop took place—to give servants the opportunity to change their employer!

Queen Elizabeth I had been on the throne for six years when William Shakespeare came into the world. As young William grew up, his interest turned to the nearby village of Shottery, to where he would walk across the fields to court Anne Hathaway, eight years his senior, whom he married when he was eighteen.

THE ROMANTIC PRESENT—pastimes for lovers...

Stratford and its surrounding countryside is a wonderful place to be in love. The area has some of the finest and most romantic gardens. The finest example of an Elizabethan knot garden can be found at **New Place**, the site of Shakespeare's last home. Here, essential culinary herbs are interwoven with flowers in a series of intricate and beautiful patterns. Boats can be hired for lazing about on the river, and in June the Avon plays host to a colourful regatta with over a hundred participators. Other special occasions include Shakespeare's **Birthday Celebrations** in April of course, and the summer **Stratford Festival**, a blend of local and international entertainment. And lastly, as there's a bit of the child left in all of us—Stratford's **Teddy Bear Museum** is a childhood dream come true.

For **lovers of food**, Stratford offers much to tempt the tastebuds. One can still find Olde English fayre, such as **Solomogundy**—a popular Elizabethan salad, **steak, kidney and oyster pie**—a dish older than Shakespeare, and **syllabub**—a wicked dessert made with whipped cream liberally laced with alcohol, lemon and spices. You may also like to sample the local **Warwickshire pudding**—a steamed pudding with a fruity cap of raspberry or apricot jam. For a romantic tipple, lovers could share a glass of mead, an old English honey liqueur. Or, for those who like to quench their thirst with a refreshing glass or two of beer, the local brew to watch out for is Flowers. Finally, what could be more pleasant after a hectic few hours' sight-seeing than to sit back and enjoy a cosy afternoon tea with your loved one? The summer strawberries on your shortbread and cream-filled scones are sure to be fresh and delicious from the famous fruit farms and orchards of the Vale of Evesham nearby.

DID YOU KNOW THAT...?

★Ontario, Canada, has its own Stratford, where it holds a distinguished Shakespeare season each summer.

★According to centuries-old tradition, St George's Day, April 23, 1564, was the day of Shakespeare's birth, and, by strange coincidence, was the day of his death in 1616.

★The building of the current theatre's Victorian predecessor was funded by local brewer Charles Flower. Not everyone liked the building. When it burned down in 1926, the playwright George Bernard Shaw sent a telegram saying simply, 'Congratulations!'

★In the gardens stretching between the theatre and Holy Trinity Church is a silver birch, planted in memory of legendary actress Vivien Leigh. A plaque is inscribed with Shakespeare's words from *Antony and Cleopatra*—'A lass unparallel'd.'

MEN MADE IN AMERICA

Fifty red-blooded, white-hot, true-blue hunks
from every State in the Union!

Look for MEN MADE IN AMERICA! Written by some of
our most popular authors, these stories feature fifty of the
strongest, sexiest men, each from a different state in the
union!

Two titles available every month at your favorite retail
outlet.

In July, look for:

ROCKY ROAD by Anne Stuart (Maine)
THE LOVE THING by Dixie Browning (Maryland)

In August, look for:

PROS AND CONS by Bethany Campbell (Massachusetts)
TO TAME A WOLF by Anne McAllister (Michigan)

You won't be able to resist MEN MADE IN AMERICA!

HARLEQUIN®

Don't miss these Harlequin favorites by some of our most
distinguished authors!
And now you can receive a discount by ordering two or more titles!

HT #25525	THE PERFECT HUSBAND by Kristine Rolofson	$2.99 ☐
HT #25554	LOVERS' SECRETS by Glenda Sanders	$2.99 ☐
HP #11577	THE STONE PRINCESS by Robyn Donald	$2.99 ☐
HP #11554	SECRET ADMIRER by Susan Napier	$2.99 ☐
HR #03277	THE LADY AND THE TOMCAT by Bethany Campbell	$2.99 ☐
HR #03283	FOREIGN AFFAIR by Eva Rutland	$2.99 ☐
HS #70529	KEEPING CHRISTMAS by Marisa Carroll	$3.39 ☐
HS #70578	THE LAST BUCCANEER by Lynn Erickson	$3.50 ☐
HI #22256	THRICE FAMILIAR by Caroline Burnes	$2.99 ☐
HI #22238	PRESUMED GUILTY by Tess Gerritsen	$2.99 ☐
HAR #16496	OH, YOU BEAUTIFUL DOLL by Judith Arnold	$3.50 ☐
HAR #16510	WED AGAIN by Elda Minger	$3.50 ☐
HH #28719	RACHEL by Lynda Trent	$3.99 ☐
HH #28795	PIECES OF SKY by Marianne Willman	$3.99 ☐

Harlequin Promotional Titles

#97122	LINGERING SHADOWS by Penny Jordan	$5.99 ☐
	(limited quantities available on certain titles)	

	AMOUNT	$
DEDUCT:	**10% DISCOUNT FOR 2+ BOOKS**	$
	POSTAGE & HANDLING	$
	($1.00 for one book, 50¢ for each additional)	
	APPLICABLE TAXES*	$_____
	TOTAL PAYABLE	$_____
	(check or money order—please do not send cash)	

To order, complete this form and send it, along with a check or money order for the
total above, payable to Harlequin Books, to: **In the U.S.:** 3010 Walden Avenue,
P.O. Box 9047, Buffalo, NY 14269-9047; **In Canada:** P.O. Box 613, Fort Erie, Ontario,
L2A 5X3.

Name: _____

Address: _____ City: _____

State/Prov.: _____ Zip/Postal Code: _____

*New York residents remit applicable sales taxes.
 Canadian residents remit applicable GST and provincial taxes..

HBACK-JS

HARLEQUIN®

Weddings, Inc.

Harlequin Books requests the pleasure of your company this June in Eternity, Massachusetts, for WEDDINGS, INC.

For generations, couples have been coming to Eternity, Massachusetts, to exchange wedding vows. Legend has it that those married in Eternity's chapel are destined for a lifetime of happiness. And the residents are more than willing to give the legend a hand.

Beginning in June, you can experience the legend of Eternity. Watch for one title per month, across all of the Harlequin series.

HARLEQUIN BOOKS... NOT THE SAME OLD STORY!

Travel across Europe in 1994
with Harlequin Presents and...

As you travel across Europe in 1994, visiting your favorite countries with your favorite authors, don't forget to collect four proofs of purchase to redeem for an appealing photo album. This photo album can hold over fifty 4"×6" pictures of your travels and will be a precious keepsake in the years to come!

One proof of purchase can be found in the back pages of each POSTCARDS FROM EUROPE title...one every month until December 1994.

To receive your gift, please fill out the information below and mail four (4) original proof-of-purchase coupons from any Harlequin Presents POSTCARDS FROM EUROPE title plus $3.00 for postage and handling (check or money order—do not send cash), payable to Harlequin Books, to: IN THE U.S.: P.O. Box 9048, Buffalo, NY, 14269-9048; IN CANADA: P.O. Box 623, Fort Erie, Ontario, L2A 5X3.

Requests must be received by January 31, 1995.
Please allow 4–6 weeks after receipt of order for delivery.

Name: _____

Address: _____

_____

City: _____

State/Province: _____

Zip/Postal Code: _____

Account No: _____

ONE PROOF OF PURCHASE

077 KBY

INDULGE A LITTLE 6947 SWEEPSTAKES
NO PURCHASE NECESSARY

HERE'S HOW THE SWEEPSTAKES WORKS:
The Harlequin Reader Service shipments for January, February and March 1994 will contain, respectively, coupons for entry into three prize drawings: a trip for two to San Francisco, an Alaskan cruise for two and a trip for two to Hawaii. To be eligible for any drawing using an Entry Coupon, simply complete and mail according to directions.

There is no obligation to continue as a Reader Service subscriber to enter and be eligible for any prize drawing. You may also enter any drawing by hand printing your name and address on a 3" x 5" card and the destination of the prize you wish that entry to be considered for (i.e., San Francisco trip, Alaskan cruise or Hawaiian trip). Send your 3" x 5" entries to: Indulge a Little 6947 Sweepstakes, c/o Prize Destination you wish that entry to be considered for, P.O. Box 1315, Buffalo, NY 14269-1315, U.S.A. or Indulge a Little 6947 Sweepstakes, P.O. Box 610, Fort Erie, Ontario L2A 5X3, Canada.

To be eligible for the San Francisco trip, entries must be received by 4/30/94; for the Alaskan cruise, 5/31/94; and the Hawaiian trip, 6/30/94. No responsibility is assumed for lost, late or misdirected mail. Sweepstakes open to residents of the U.S. (except Puerto Rico) and Canada, 18 years of age or older. All applicable laws and regulations apply. Sweepstakes void wherever prohibited.

For a copy of the Official Rules, send a self-addressed, stamped envelope (WA residents need not affix return postage) to: Indulge a Little 6947 Rules, P.O. Box 4631, Blair, NE 68009, U.S.A.

INDR93

INDULGE A LITTLE 6947 SWEEPSTAKES
NO PURCHASE NECESSARY

HERE'S HOW THE SWEEPSTAKES WORKS:
The Harlequin Reader Service shipments for January, February and March 1994 will contain, respectively, coupons for entry into three prize drawings: a trip for two to San Francisco, an Alaskan cruise for two and a trip for two to Hawaii. To be eligible for any drawing using an Entry Coupon, simply complete and mail according to directions.

There is no obligation to continue as a Reader Service subscriber to enter and be eligible for any prize drawing. You may also enter any drawing by hand printing your name and address on a 3" x 5" card and the destination of the prize you wish that entry to be considered for (i.e., San Francisco trip, Alaskan cruise or Hawaiian trip). Send your 3" x 5" entries to: Indulge a Little 6947 Sweepstakes, c/o Prize Destination you wish that entry to be considered for, P.O. Box 1315, Buffalo, NY 14269-1315, U.S.A. or Indulge a Little 6947 Sweepstakes, P.O. Box 610, Fort Erie, Ontario L2A 5X3, Canada.

To be eligible for the San Francisco trip, entries must be received by 4/30/94; for the Alaskan cruise, 5/31/94; and the Hawaiian trip, 6/30/94. No responsibility is assumed for lost, late or misdirected mail. Sweepstakes open to residents of the U.S. (except Puerto Rico) and Canada, 18 years of age or older. All applicable laws and regulations apply. Sweepstakes void wherever prohibited.

For a copy of the Official Rules, send a self-addressed, stamped envelope (WA residents need not affix return postage) to: Indulge a Little 6947 Rules, P.O. Box 4631, Blair, NE 68009, U.S.A.

INDR93

※※※INDULGE A LITTLE※※※
SWEEPSTAKES

OFFICIAL ENTRY COUPON

This entry must be received by: JUNE 30, 1994
This month's winner will be notified by: JULY 15, 1994
Trip must be taken between: AUGUST 31, 1994-AUGUST 31, 1995

YES, I want to win the 3-Island Hawaiian vacation for two. I understand that the prize includes round-trip airfare, first-class hotels and pocket money as revealed on the "wallet" scratch-off card.

Name_____

Address _____ Apt. _____

City_____

State/Prov._____ Zip/Postal Code_____

Daytime phone number_____
                              (Area Code)

Account #_____

Return entries with invoice in envelope provided. Each book in this shipment has two entry coupons—and the more coupons you enter, the better your chances of winning!
© 1993 HARLEQUIN ENTERPRISES LTD.   MONTH3

※※※INDULGE A LITTLE※※※
SWEEPSTAKES

OFFICIAL ENTRY COUPON

This entry must be received by: JUNE 30, 1994
This month's winner will be notified by: JULY 15, 1994
Trip must be taken between: AUGUST 31, 1994-AUGUST 31, 1995

YES, I want to win the 3-Island Hawaiian vacation for two. I understand that the prize includes round-trip airfare, first-class hotels and pocket money as revealed on the "wallet" scratch-off card.

Name_____

Address _____ Apt. _____

City_____

State/Prov._____ Zip/Postal Code_____

Daytime phone number_____
                              (Area Code)

Account #_____

Return entries with invoice in envelope provided. Each book in this shipment has two entry coupons—and the more coupons you enter, the better your chances of winning!
© 1993 HARLEQUIN ENTERPRISES LTD.   MONTH3